"A fun and exciting book! I loved it as much as the first. Makes the Deep Ellum neighborhood sound so magical, and I was swept away by the magic of the musical characters as well! Can't wait for the next one to come out!" -- Goodreads Review

"G. S. Norwood's magic sizzles and sparks again in Deep Ellum Blues. After having been introduced to the remarkable Eddy Weekes in Deep Ellum Pawn, I was more than eager to follow along on her next adventure. The sequel does not disappoint." -- Amazon Review

"Unique Story...And a very entertaining story as well. Eddy is a very different kind of goddess, and if you have read the first story, then I am not giving away any secrets. If you haven't read 'Deep Ellum Pawn," then why not?" -- Goodreads Review

"Deep Ellum Blues hits all the notes. Urban Fantasy, check. Good and evil, check. Interesting characters, check. And tons of good music (if you hear the music in your head when you read, like I do! If you don't......there's even a playlist for later!) G. S. Norwood is a must read for everyone." -- Amazon Review

Praise for G. S. Norwood's Deep Ellum Stories

Authors Honor the "Deep Ellum" Series!

"Some of the best stories I've ever read!"

—Elizabeth Ann Scarborough, Nebula Award-winning author of *The Healer's War*.

"G. S. Norwood is a mesmerizing new voice in urban fantasy. If you love Ben Aaronovitch you'll love **Deep Ellum Pawn!**"

—Deborah Crombie, New York Times bestselling author of the "Kincaid and James" series

"**Deep Ellum Blues** reaches beyond the old stories to reveal that the true power of the Blues is rooted not in darkness and damnation, but in redemption and light . . . Somewhere, Blind Lemon Jefferson and T-Bone Walker are smiling."

—Bradley Denton, author of *Buddy Holly is Alive and Well on Ganymede*

Readers Love "Deep Ellum Pawn"!

"Wonderful little gem of a story: This novelette left me satisfied, but wanting more. I can't wait to see what else makes its way into Deep Ellum Pawn in the future!" — Amazon Review

"A lovely little novella, good dialect and beautiful story." — Goodreads Review

"A very entertaining read: A wonderful story full of rich

detail. Totally taken by pleasant surprise by the turns into the supernatural. Ready for more!" — Amazon Review

"Miz Eddy is awesome! This little story is an urban fantasy gem. Just want more!" — Goodreads Review

"An entertaining story well told. Ms. Eddy is a joy and I look forward to reading more about her." — Amazon Review

Readers Praise "Deep Ellum Blues"!

"Wow. I'm blown away by how much I enjoyed this little escape of a novelette. The language is so evocative, I felt like I was actually there. The author's detailed knowledge of music and instruments added so much depth. I spent a lot of the 90s in Deep Ellum supporting a friend's band. This story brought back so many memories of that time. I can't wait for the next little slice of life in Deep Ellum to be released." -- Goodreads Review

"The second Deep Ellum novella by G.S.Norwood, whose love of urban fantasy, blues music, and the iconic Dallas neighborhood of Deep Ellum resonate in every word. Whether you're a blues fan or not, the magic in this story is sure to rattle your bones." --Amazon Review

"What fun to return to Deep Ellum, and the company of Ms. Eddy! She has a new puzzle to unravel after a friend sends her a cryptic text. But an interesting puzzle becomes a deeper kind of danger when she realizes who is doing his best to influence a talented musician onto a deadly path." -- Goodreads Review

"I've never been in the Deep Ellum section of Dallas but I feel as though I know the mood of the place from descriptions of Eddy walking through the streets." --Amazon Review

Deep Ellum Duet

---

*Two Urban Fantasy Novelettes: Deep Ellum
Pawn and Deep Ellum Blues*

Deep Ellum Stories

G. S. Norwood

Contents

Everyday Magic
By G. S. Norwood

I believe in magic. Not the David Copperfield, big stage illusion kind. Not the Harry Potter wave-a-wand-and-say-the-right-words kind. I believe in the natural kind that arises from the energy shared by people who gather around a common belief.

You've probably felt that energy yourself, humming through a crowd of grandparents, parents, grand and great-grandchildren all gathered together to watch the latest movie in the Star Wars saga. Maybe you hold your breath for that brief instant at the start of a concert or a play, before the baton gives the downbeat or the curtain goes up. If you gasped along with the little ones as the snowflakes began to fall at the end of the first act of *The Nutcracker*, you have felt it. It's the energy that whispers amazing things are possible, and Tinkerbell will survive, if only we believe.

To write urban fantasy, as I do, you have to believe that kind of life-force energy hums just under the surface of even the grittiest city. You may need to peel back the layers of concrete and asphalt right down to the dirt, then call on the folklore and fairy tales, old songs and old wives' tales that have grown up around a place to find it. Then you must weave in history and legend until the story has one foot in reality, and one foot in fantasy.

My novelette, *Deep Ellum Pawn*, began with that mix of practicality and possibility. I had an old Charlie Daniels song stuck in my mind. *The Devil Went Down to Georgia* is catchy, but I couldn't help but wonder why anyone would want a fiddle made of gold. Gold is a dense metal, heavy to hold, and not very resonant. A golden fiddle—particularly one from the Devil himself—would likely sound less than musical. So, what do you do with it? Melt it down? Take it to a pawn shop?

The moment that thought popped into my mind a character followed. That's how I met Ms. Eddy Weekes, proprietress of Deep Ellum Pawn. It's a dusty pawn shop in one of Dallas' oldest neighborhoods, but there's more going on behind the façade than anyone might suspect.

The story flowed quickly, and I began to wonder if I'd made it up, or if some force beyond my imagination was prompting me to write it all down the way it "really" happened. Every time I paused to research a new plot point, I found not only the answer I was looking for, but reams of additional information that made the whole idea even richer and deeper.

For example, hellhounds make an appearance in the story. And why not? Deep Ellum is only a few short blocks from the building where bluesman Robert Johnson recorded his song, *Hellhound on My Trail*. Johnson himself gave me my first clue about how to manage hellhounds when his lyrics mentioned hotfoot powder—a folk charm used to harden the threshold of a home against supernatural invaders. A bit further down the hellhound trail I learned that to look one in the eye three times means death. Great stuff for an urban fantasist.

The dance halls and street corners of Deep Ellum gave American blues legends besides Robert Johnson an early career boost. The Sons of Hermann Hall has hunched on the corner of Elm Street and Exposition for more than 100 years, and remains the oldest continuously operating bar and music venue in Dallas. The string bands and bluesmen who played Deep Ellum in the early 20th century gave way to swing bands and later the singer-songwriters who created Americana music. We have no actual record of Robert Johnson playing there, but we do know that Blind Lemon Jefferson, T-Bone Walker, Stevie Ray Vaughan, and countless others took the stage in this little corner of Dallas. Dave Grohl, in his memoir *The Storyteller*, recalls an early gig with Nirvana that surely had Ms. Eddy's fingerprints all over it. My novelette *Deep Ellum Blues* draws on that strand of history to spin a tale of what might happen when Ms. Eddy takes a personal interest in one such musician.

Deep Ellum Pawn and *Deep Ellum Blues* were originally published in e-book format only, but many readers wanted a book they could hold in their hands. A "real" book. That's why Weird Sisters Publishing decided to come out with *Deep Ellum Duet*. This small volume combines the two novelettes, so you can read them in order, and enjoy a paper-based format. Either way, when different ideas, drawn from history, folklore, and my own imagination, all fall together to make a coherent and entertaining whole, that feels like magic to me.

I hope it will feel like magic to you, too.

DEEP ELLUM PAWN
G. S. NORWOOD

Deep Ellum Pawn - The First Novelette

By G. S. Norwood

*This story is dedicated
to the memory of Warren C. Norwood,
who first introduced me to
the history and magic of Deep Ellum.*

Golden Fiddle
Chapter One

The guy on the other side of the counter shifted from foot to foot, taking quick swipes at his streaming nose with the cuff of his beige flannel shirt. His eyes, half-hidden by greasy blond bangs, darted from side to side, as if he was afraid Hell Hounds would appear at any moment, hot on his trail.

God knows, the Hounds wouldn't have any trouble following his scent. He reeked of sweat, adrenaline, and old urine.

I looked from him to the battered violin case he'd shoved across my sales counter toward me. I was pretty sure what I'd find inside.

"Two hundred bucks," I said.

"You haven't even looked at it!"

"One fifty."

"But it's *gold*!"

Of course it was. "One hundred. Take it or leave it."

"That's not fair! It's worth lots more than that! You don't understand!"

I did understand. I understood that all his hopes and fears were in that case. Maybe even his life's meaning. I understood that he wanted his lost dreams and wasted talent to be worth more than one hundred measly dollars. I also understood that he was really, really bad at striking bargains.

"Look, buddy." I leaned closer despite the waves of meth sweat wafting off of him. "You used to be a musician, right?"

"I AM a musician!" He tried to stand up straighter, but some old pain caught him between the shoulder blades and he hunched over again. "I played with the Dallas Symphony."

"Uh-huh. And you were pretty good. Then some guy challenged you to a fiddling contest, which you won, and he gave you his fiddle as the prize." I rested my hand on the duct tape that covered the violin case. "This fiddle, which is made of solid gold."

Heat, and a faint vibration, rose up from the case as if the instrument inside was alive.

"It has no resonance. The strings screech like damned souls. And ever since you got it, you've had horrible nightmares about giant, slavering bloodhounds with eyes red as fire, tracking you down to carry your soul to Hell."

My gaze held his as the color leached from his face.

"The booze didn't help, and neither did the pills." I counted down the steps. "So you tried the harder stuff. You lost your chair at the symphony, then your cushy apartment, your equally cushy girlfriend, and now even your mother won't accept your calls. Maybe I'm a sap, but I will take this cursed instrument off your hands and give you dreamless sleep, room to breathe, and one last chance to turn your life around. Plus fifty bucks."

He blinked. "Fifty bucks?"

"That's enough to buy you something to eat and a cab to

the rehab facility of your choice. I'm giving you your freedom, asshole. You should be paying me."

He nodded once, and took a step back as I counted out the bills. His fingers didn't touch mine as he snatched his money and bolted out the door.

He didn't need to run. The Hell Hounds were my problem now.

A brisk wind kicked a shower of red-gold leaves down the street as he disappeared into the swirl of hipsters and hucksters who called Deep Ellum home.

At two o'clock on a cool fall afternoon, the lunch crowd had pretty much disappeared from my little pocket of Dallas. The pub crawlers had yet to show up, but the natives were out in their usual force. A steady parade of beards, body piercings, green hair, and tattoo sleeves surged past my pawn shop windows.

I looked tame in comparison. These days I wore my hair longer, without a hint of purple or pink, and favored trim jeans and loose flannel shirts to the flamboyantly patterned leggings and mini-skirts the Deep Ellum fashionistas preferred. No makeup, so anyone who cared to look could see the full, rich blend of Black, Native American, and Anglo written boldly across my face.

It was a face that reflected the neighborhood. A century ago Deep Ellum had been the heart of Dallas' Black business community, and pawn shops had lined every block. Today, mine was the only pawn shop left, wedged in amongst the pizza parlors, leather shops, and music clubs. The people were a more diverse mix, but Deep Ellum was still a place you could find just about any type of trouble you wanted to get into.

The legendary bluesman, Robert Johnson, had recorded his song about Hell Hounds on his trail just a few blocks west of here. I looked down at the ragged violin case on my counter. "What kind of song are you trying to sing?" I asked the fiddle softly.

Rather than speculate, I dug my utility knife out of my back pocket and got to work. Duct tape all but mummified the case. Its former owner had used far more than was necessary if he just wanted to keep the case from falling open. No. He'd wanted to make sure the thing stayed shut.

With a little effort, I peeled back enough layers of tape to get a look at the case itself. It was made of wood, covered by leather, and there were scorch marks along the seam where the top met the bottom, as if there had once been a fire inside.

"Great," I muttered as I pried it open. I should have worn gloves. My fingers were already sticking together.

But there it was, just as I remembered it. The fiddle was heartbreakingly beautiful and light as a feather, despite being made of solid gold. As I lifted it out of the case, a stray afternoon sunbeam broke through the burglar bars on my front window to dance along the silver strings.

There was a matching bow, perfectly balanced, that seemed to adjust itself to my hand as I held it over the strings. Ripples of energy passed between the two, all but begging me to touch bow to fiddle and make some music. Any music. Irish jigs, bluegrass breakdowns, classical sonatas, Iron Maiden covers; whatever I chose, it would be glorious.

"Fat chance, fiddle freak." I said the words aloud, with a snarl of contempt, just in case anyone was listening. Nobody needed to know how strongly I was tempted.

I put bow and fiddle back in the case and closed the lid, then stepped away. Took a deep breath and let it out slowly as my gaze wandered over my pawn shop. It was kind of a jumble, as pawn shops get to be. Everything from gas-powered weed eaters to old videotapes—even a prosthetic leg—filled the shelves in the center of the room. A dozen guitars and a couple of fiddles hung from the wall to my right, with amps, drums, and a symphonic gong arranged neatly underneath.

Two glass cases of jewelry—mostly wedding rings—stood against the wall to my left. I kept some guns in a display case on the end wall, with the rest locked in a safe behind it.

You'd think anyone who wanted to rob a pawn shop would go for the guns or the jewelry, but the only thing ever stolen from my place was this damn golden fiddle. Three times, in fact. And the hell of it was, people just kept bringing it back.

Something brushed against my leg and I looked down into the green eyes of a small black cat.

"Hey, Tid," I greeted her. "Where you been? The fiddle is back."

I'd rescued Tidbit, along with her brother, Morsel, from the dumpster behind the 7- Eleven several years back. They were full-time residents of the pawn shop, just like me. Morsel spent his days roaming the alleys and wasting his charm on the girls from the charter school over on Elm. Tid stayed closer to home, focusing her efforts on keeping my shop free of rats and mice. I liked that in a cat.

She leapt up onto the counter with the easy grace of one who wastes no time on nonsense like golden violins. Butted her head into my hand. This meant that she loved me, but her bowl was empty, and if I loved her, I'd attend to it right away.

I did love her, so I stretched my arms above my head, rolled my shoulders to work out the tension, then followed Tid back to the kitchen in the private part of the shop. I left the violin case on the counter—a straight shot in from the door. No way you could miss it if you happened to glance in from the street. Maybe someone else would steal it.

I should be so lucky.

Assay Test
Chapter Two

Of course the damned violin was still on the counter when I got back from feeding Tid. I stared at the scorched, peeling, sticky case for a few moments, hoping for inspiration, before I realized I had forgotten my own lunch. "Running low on energy, Eddy," I muttered to myself. "That's why you're stuck."

Not that I expected a bit of sustenance would bring me lightning bolts of brilliance, but a walk in the sunshine always lifted my spirits. I promised myself I'd tackle the fiddle just as soon as I got back, grabbed my hoodie, and stepped out into the world.

There was a nip in the wind. I ran a quick check on the front of my store as I zipped my jacket. The wrought iron burglar bars were rust-free. Nothing broken or shorted out on the neon "Deep Ellum Pawn" sign over the door. The hand-carved desk, freshly-painted doghouse, and slightly dented tuba in the front window would intrigue customers. A sign, made by a loyal customer, was clearly visible from the sidewalk.

"Honest Eddy Weekes," it said. The sign bore a smiling

cartoon figure of a curvy young woman who was probably meant to be me. "Here when you need her." A throng of happy cartoon people surrounded the woman with speech balloons over their heads that read, "Thank you, Eddy!" and "We believe in you!"

It all looked good. With a nod, I headed past the fluttering streamers of the tattoo parlor on the corner, then cut over to Commerce Street to wind past the burger joints and bars to my favorite sandwich shop.

About halfway along, I spotted a cluster of young creatives near the former flophouse that was now a shared-space office complex. They'd stepped outside to smoke, or vape, or whatever they did when they wanted to get up from their desks and take a brain break.

"Hey, Eddy!" A cute brunette, with pixie-short hair and a pixie-short dress, waved as I got close.

"Pomona. Aren't you cold in this wind?" I nodded at her bare legs.

"Nah." She wrapped her little cardigan more tightly around her torso, as if that would keep her knees from turning blue, and pulled a tall, shaggy sapling of a guy out of the knot of her co-workers. "Michael, this is Eddy. She owns the pawn shop I told you about. You should go there. She has guitars."

"You a musician?" I asked. "I have amps, too. Drums. Lots of stuff. Come in anytime, if you're interested."

Michael did not look particularly interested, but Pomona gave it one more shot. "Eddy is a great supporter of the arts. Show her what you're doing. She's bound to love it. She said wonderful things to me when I showed her my portfolio."

"That's because you're talented," I said. "I believe in you."

"I believe in you, too, Eddy!" Pomona grinned and tipped me a wink.

"And right now, I believe in lunch." I nodded to them both

as I turned away. "Nice to meet you, Michael." He'd be in, I figured, but he'd be looking at rings, not amps. At least if Pomona got her way. I believed in her on that front, too.

A couple of cop cars sat at the curb by the sandwich shop. It was one of the reasons I frequented the place. It never hurt to foster friendly relations with our emergency responders. Plus, they had all the good gossip.

"Eddy!" Two extra-large police officers—one Black and one brown—greeted me as I squeezed into the extra-small shop. I had to twist sideways to reach the counter without jostling their holstered pistols.

"Gentlemen," I responded. "How's the day treating you?"

"So far, so good," said Officer Stokes, the brown one, who came by once a week to pick up the police copies of all my pawn tickets.

"Only excitement was some junkie collapsed over on Malcolm X about thirty minutes ago." Officer Gilmore's bass rumble would have made an earthquake proud. "White guy. Scruffy beard. Beige flannel shirt. You ever see him around?"

Violin Guy. I needed to be careful here. He hadn't filled out a ticket on the golden fiddle. Yet. "Greasy blond hair? Bad teeth?"

When Stokes and Gilmore nodded, I nodded back. "Yeah, he came in just after noon. Had a crappy old fiddle he wanted to sell me." I was pretty sure I had one of those in the back if they asked. "Claimed it was made of solid gold. I figured he was high on something."

"You gave him money, didn't you?" A wide grin split Stokes' face. "For what? Food and a trip to rehab?"

"You sayin' I'm a soft touch, Officer Stokes?"

"I believe in your generous heart, Ms. Weekes."

"Yeah. Well. I might have given him something. He looked like he was all stove-in."

"Told you that fifty came from her." Stokes opened his palm to Gilmore, who put a ten in it without comment.

"What did he do? Buy a hit and OD?" I hoped not.

"Nope. Just collapsed from bein' sick, hungry, and miserable, as far as we could tell," Stokes said.

"Ambulance took him to Baylor," Gilmore added. "He'll probably live."

"Until the next time." Stokes didn't look optimistic.

I paid for my sandwich, wished the two officers and the three folks behind the counter a good day, and headed north toward Elm Street.

A new building was going up across from the bondage and leatherwear shop. They'd taken out a whole block of crumbling storefronts from the 1940s to build a high-rise condo complex. I figured that meant a new wave of gentrification was about to hit Deep Ellum, even worse than the plague of pricey lofts and fern bars that hit in the 1990s.

A few Chamber of Commerce types were gathered on the sidewalk in front of the construction. An equal number of natives watched and muttered from the sidewalk in front of the leather shop. Looked like C of C Suit #1 was giving the rest of the suits some kind of sales pitch.

" . . . Because we believe in preserving and promoting the unique spirit of this historic neighborhood!" His voice carried across the street as I came up behind the unreceptive crew of locals.

"Preserving and promoting my ass," said the tank-sized woman in white tee and black leather pants.

"It's a fine ass, Violet. You gotta admit."

Violet, whose mohawked hair matched her name, turned my way, and her frown turned even fiercer. "Why don't you do something, Eddy? You've been here longer than anyone. They should listen to you."

I shrugged. "Neighborhoods change, Violet. But I don't plan on going anywhere."

"Gawd, I hope not. It wouldn't be Deep Ellum without you."

I slid around her with a smile and crossed on a diagonal to avoid the C of C guys. A few more blocks brought me to the 7-Eleven, where I found Perkins, one of our resident homeless guys, leaning against the wall next to the dumpster, smoking a cigarette.

"Hey, Perkins." I handed him my sandwich, which he accepted, but didn't so much as look at. "See Morsel anywhere lately? I hear there's a pack of dogs comin' around at night. I don't want him to be caught out."

"Ain't seen no dogs," Perkins said. "Heard 'em, though. Last night."

"Don't you be caught out, either."

"I got me a place. No worries."

"Know anything about a skinny little blond guy, claims he has a golden fiddle?"

"That dude's messed up." Perkins had been an on-the-street alcoholic for at least two years, with intermittent bouts of the DTs and the occasional psychotic break. He knew messed up when he saw it. "Showed up last night, askin' about you. Heard them dogs 'bout an hour later."

So Violin Guy had come to Deep Ellum from somewhere outside, looking for me in particular. Interesting.

"Cops took the guy to Baylor just now," I said. "Dogs may be a little harder to get rid of." Might as well warn him one more time. If the Hell Hounds were coming, I didn't want any collateral damage.

"Saw old Morse' about an hour ago, over by the school." Perkins ground out his cigarette on the sole of his shoe. "I'll be sure to send him home if I see him again."

"'Preciate it." I nodded as I turned back toward my shop.

"Keep on believin', Ms. Eddy." Perkins called after me. "That's what I do."

And still nobody had stolen the violin.

I stared at it, drumming my fingers on the counter. I filled out a pawn ticket, using a fake name and fictional address for Violin Guy, and described the object he'd pawned simply as "old violin, poor condition." Then I filed the ticket so it would be there when Stokes came around, fetched a cracked old fiddle out of the trove of junk in the back as a stand-in, and carried the golden fiddle, sticky case and all, into my private office behind the kitchen.

The front of the store might look like your average, cluttered pawn shop, but back here I had cushioned floors, excellent lighting, and state-of-the-art equipment. Also soundproofed walls and a few other amenities the general public didn't need to know about. I put the fiddle on my workbench, and got out my tools. Of course, I had done all this the first time the fiddle came into my store. And the second. And the third. But due diligence needs to be done, no matter how many times it takes.

First, I centered the violin under my brightest light, and got out my jeweler's loupe. Examining the instrument inch by inch, I looked for any clues as to who made it. Golden objects are supposed to have hallmarks stamped into them. This thing had nothing. I put away the loupe, got out my toolbox, and selected my finest file. A little scrape just below the end button wouldn't be too noticeable, but it didn't matter. The file slid over the violin like glass, leaving nary a nick or scrape. Which made it really hard to try the next test—the acid test—on gold shavings.

Pretty sure I already knew how it would turn out, I opened my acid bottle and dabbed the tiniest drop on the place I had tried to scrape. If it turned green, the fiddle was some kind of gold-colored junk. If it turned black, the fiddle was gold.

The acid sat on the surface like a drop of water. Annoyed, I decided to skip all the "how much gold is in this alloy" tests and get down to basics. I picked up my oxygen propane torch and lit the propane, turning the soft yellow flame blue as I added oxygen to the mix. Then I pointed the torch at the violin, moving the flame in little circles over the scroll.

I didn't take precautions like heating a dish to receive the gold as it melted, because I knew it wasn't going to melt. As it had before, the violin stayed perfectly intact. I got the feeling I could run over it with a train, and the damned thing would come out whole. I might have tested the theory except I was afraid it would derail the train.

"So what are you?" I asked the fiddle. "Clearly not gold. Adamantium, like Wolverine's claws?"

I decided to go to an expert.

"Hey," I said to the weary-sounding woman who answered the phone. "Tell Waylon it's Eddy Weekes."

Waylon Smith ran a honky-tonk way out west of Fort Worth, in Heller, Texas. I'd lost track of all the promising young musicians he'd discovered in that dance hall. In an earlier life he'd run a 24-hour wrecker service, and before all that, he'd been a goldsmith. I'd met him eons ago, when some punk stole the wedding ring Waylon had made for his first wife, and he'd come in to see if it had been pawned.

"Eddy?" His voice hadn't changed. It still sounded warm, gruff, and slightly scratchy, as if he didn't use it enough.

"The golden fiddle is back, and it's definitely not gold. I

can't scratch it. Acid won't touch it. I can't even melt it. Could you take a look? See what you can do?"

"If it keeps coming back to you, I'd say you're the one who's meant to deal with it," Waylon could have been explaining to a small child. "My lookin' won't change a thing."

"But what do I do with it? I don't even know what it's made of."

"Sure you do." I could hear his impatience a hundred miles away. "Think a minute. What is more immutable than gold?"

"God damn it!"

"Maybe. But maybe not. Guess that's what you need to find out." He hung up before I could thank him.

Not that I wanted to.

He'd told me the one thing I absolutely did not want to hear. The cursed fiddle was made of an immutable human soul.

Hell Hounds

Chapter Three

Darkness had fallen while I was messing with the violin. I opened the front door of the shop and checked the situation on the street. The guy who owned the scooter place down the block was moving his bikes in for the night. We waved. Traffic had picked up as the over-privileged youth of Dallas filtered into Deep Ellum, looking for the newest edgy nightclub or a favorite dive bar.

Neon signs for those places flickered to life as I turned my sign off. A patch of shadow slid along the front of the building and darted through the door just as I pulled it shut.

"Nice of you to make it home, Morsel."

The cat, who was at least four times bigger than his sister, barely flicked an ear my way before he headed for his food bowl in the back.

I shot the deadbolt, but lingered a moment longer.

It would not do to have Hell Hounds baying at my front door. The sidewalks in this part of Deep Ellum stayed busy until sometime after 2 a.m. A pack of howling, slavering bloodhounds with eyes that burned like fire would attract attention. Freak folks out.

And then what would they do? Call Animal Control? Hell Hounds are hard to catch, impossible to put down, and not exactly adoptable, since they're supposed to be omens of death.

It would cause problems. People might get hurt. Hell Hounds might get hurt, for that matter, and they'd probably slobber all over my front windows in the melee. It would be a mess no matter how I looked at it. Better to avoid the whole situation.

I decided some folk remedies might be the answer, and I figured I had just what I needed in my back garden.

My building was bigger when it was built in the 1920s. Local legend said it had been a brothel, or a speakeasy, or maybe both. The two-story storefront, with the pawn shop at ground level and my apartment above, hadn't changed, but a one-story extension had once jutted out from what was now my kitchen-office-lab area. That extension had caught fire sometime in the late 1930s. Nothing but the sturdy brick walls still stood.

I'd ripped up the concrete floor, gone down to good, healthy Deep Ellum soil, and turned the whole area into an enclosed garden. Rock-paved paths wound around a little central lawn, with raised beds of native Texas plants along the sides. My table and chair sat beside a little pool where I liked to catch up with the news every morning. A double-wide privacy gate closed off the far end from the alley behind.

As the moon rose over Deep Ellum, I walked along the paths, snipping a little Texas sage and picking a few of the ornamental peppers that poked up like thin red fingers from a pot of pretty leaves. At the gate I untangled a handful of wild morning glory vine to add to my supplies.

The rest of the stuff I'd need was in the shop or the kitchen.

I still had work to do, before the Hell Hounds found me.

Just around midnight, I heard the first snuffles and scrapes out in the alley, on the other side of my garden gate. Morsel and Tid must have heard it, too. Morse faded into the shadows under the little patio table beside me, while Tid took cover behind a cluster of pepper plants in one of the raised beds.

I couldn't see what was in the alley but the noises were distinctly doggy. And maybe a little puzzled, as if they thought they were in the right place, but couldn't quite find the scent. Lots of panting and pacing back and forth. A soft yip, or low snarl.

Mindful of the busy street out front and the tendency of drunken young folks to wander into dark alleys, I decided to give the Hounds a hand. The violin rested in its case on the table beside me, next to a large pottery bowl. I flipped the case open, and a little breeze wafted over it, stirring the strings.

The howl went up in the alley almost immediately. There's no mistaking Hell Hounds in full cry—the deep-throated bay of a bloodhound mixed with the keen of a wolf and the snarl of a feral dog, eager to kill something more challenging than chickens.

So. Definitely Hell Hounds. Time to get the party started.

A quick nod, and my back gate flew open. The Hounds spilled through like a flood of ink. Their eyes really did burn red with the fires of Hell, and those eyes were fixed on me. Blood and foam dripped from their muzzles, and they had a whole lot of genuinely fearsome, razor sharp teeth.

It was a pretty impressive display. More than enough to give Violin Guy nightmares, or scare a gentle soul like Perkins half to death. They rushed across my lawn as I stood behind my pool, my bare feet planted on the ground.

But the Hounds pulled up sharply just the other side of my pool, as if they'd run smack into a wall they couldn't see. The hounds at the back of the pack plowed into their leaders, then leapt away, only to bounce off that invisible barrier at the side of the lawn. As the last one bounded through the gate, the whole pack began to mill and mutter to themselves. They never took their eyes off of me, but they clearly didn't know how to reach my side and rip out my throat.

Score one for Robert Johnson. His song plus a bit of research had given me the recipe for hotfoot power. The mixture of sage, salt, cayenne pepper, and gunpowder kept the Hounds at bay. I'd thrown in the morning glory vine to make it a tad more binding, then circled the lawn with it, leaving a gap at the gate so they could get in. And out again.

The pack leader shook his head and his lips curled back, as if he'd tasted something nasty. Then he growled low in his throat, letting his voice rise to a howl of rage.

The others joined in an angry chorus. There were nine of them, and I could see now they were a mixed lot: some bloodhounds, as I'd expected, but also three I would have called yellow curs if they hadn't been solid black. The leader looked like a giant ebony timber wolf, with his long wedge of a snout, triangular ears, and impressively shaggy ruff.

As one, they rushed forward again, crashing into the hotfoot powder boundary I had drawn.

I set my feet more firmly in the earth and jerked my chin up a fraction.

The gunpowder ignited, fizzing and sparking all around them, ringing them in, with only one way to escape. The Hounds tried to scramble away, hampered by the tight space of the lawn. They packed themselves into a wary knot in the center of the grass, away from the fire that showed no sign of dying down.

I tipped my hands slightly to either side, and the pool at my feet deepened and spread, widening to form a broad crescent that circled half the lawn along my side of the hotfoot line. Something the size of a river otter flowed past, just beneath the surface, and disappeared into the depths.

The lead Hound watched the ripples die away, then met my eyes directly. The fire in his eyes flashed, but I sensed fear beneath the defiance.

I nodded again, and the gate crashed shut.

The Hounds began to bay once more, but this time I heard an edge of panic. They scrambled over each other, fighting to get back to the gate. But it was coated with hotfoot power too.

Yipping and snarling, they turned on each other, snapping at throats and necks, ripping at legs and ears.

"Enough!" I shouted over their noise.

They froze in place.

"Sit!"

All nine of them sat. Who knew the Devil believed in obedience training?

"I have a message for your master."

All ears pricked to catch my words.

"He sent you here to claim this violin and the soul of the person who had it." I focused on the pack leader, whose gaze never wavered from mine. It looked like he'd taken some damage in the fight. Blood matted one of his ears and smeared his face below one eye. He held his right front paw up as if it was too painful to put weight on it.

"You tell him this violin is mine. The case is mine. The bow is mine. If he wants it, he can come bargain for it himself. I'll be here when he's ready."

The gate snapped open behind them. "Now go on! Git!"

I reached into the bowl and grabbed a handful of raw hamburger from the meat market over on Elm. Freshly ground, it still oozed blood. The Hounds caught the scent as I lobbed about a pound of it over their heads into the alley.

The Hounds rose to their feet, noses in the air.

That was the moment Morsel chose to make his entrance. Secure in his lair under the table, he had grown to the size he always believed he should be, which turned out to be about as big as a Bengal tiger.

Surging out of the darkness, he leapt the pool and pounced on the nearest Hound. He sank his teeth into the dog's spine and I heard something crunch as he slammed its body into the ground. My cat roared in victory.

The other Hounds backed away, licking their lips and glancing at each other.

"Git!" I yelled again, and threw another pound of meat.

The remaining Hell Hounds swiveled toward the gate and bolted, chasing their freedom and what might have been the first good meal they'd had lately.

Tid, now the size of a large ocelot, sprang from her hiding place in the flowerbed, landing on the last Hound in the pack. Her front claws sank into the Hound's shoulder while her back claws raked his leg.

He twisted sideways, shrieking with panic.

Tid rode him all the way to the gate, then dropped off as he fled into the alley. Without a backward glance, she minced back into the garden as the din of the Hell Hounds faded into the distance.

Morsel still stood over the body of his prey. I watched as the dead Hell Hound dissolved into ashes and blew away, following its pack mates toward the Trinity River.

"Don't worry, Morse'," I told him. "I have a nice can of tuna for you in the kitchen."

A soft growl told us we weren't quite done with the Hell Hounds yet. I scanned the garden. Down near the base of a planter I spotted the pack leader.

He rose from the ground and limped forward, until he stood directly across from me, on the far side of my pool. His eyes locked on mine.

Now, folklorists will tell you that to meet the gaze of a Hell Hound three times means certain, immediate death. They just aren't real clear on who or what will die. I saw the pain in the Hound's eyes as the hellfire died out. It dwindled to a dull orange glow that faded into the golden eyes of a normal dog. His massive body shrank from something taller and heavier than an Irish Wolfhound to the size of a large Siberian Husky.

He raised his injured paw and whimpered.

"What's the matter, bud? You slip your chain and lose your master?"

Slowly, creakily, the dog stretched forward into an awkward play bow, then rolled his eyes up to mine, as if to see if I was buying his pitiful act.

Tid, who had shrunk back down to her normal size, stalked up to him, sniffed his injured paw, then strolled away, nose in the air. Morsel, who seemed in no hurry to abandon his tiger size, walked past without so much as a glance.

Dog people have sworn to me that the dog picks his master, not the other way around. I had the feeling I had just been chosen.

"All right, then." I jerked my head toward the gate, which snapped shut. The pool began to flow back into itself, resuming its former shape. The ripple within it sank away with the swish of a fluked tail. I closed the violin case, tucked it under my arm, and picked up the bowl of meat.

The garden had returned to its normal state and was once more at peace.

"You comin'?" I asked the former Hell Hound.

The dog rose from his bow. His tail tilted slightly from one side to the other, as if it didn't quite remember how to wag. Stepping over the hotfoot powder boundary and skirting the pool, he followed me into the shop.

Ace in the Hole

Chapter Four

I figured the former Hell Hound would need something better than a steady diet of raw hamburger and human souls so, come morning, I took him down to the dog place on Elm at Central. They had all kinds of stuff for the pampered pooches who live in Deep Ellum's lofts. The building had once housed one of the neighborhood's best pawn shops. Seeing Honest Joe's all decked out for dog grooming and daycare always made me a little sad.

I wasn't sure how far I could trust the former Hell Hound, but running away seemed to be the last thing on his mind. He walked right beside me all the way to the store, as if he'd been trained to heel. Which, I suppose, he more or less had been. I don't guess his former master tolerated much deviation from the main agenda.

I was happy to note that, although the Hound took great interest in the buildings and people we passed along the way, he appeared to have lost his compulsion to track down sinners and drag them to Hell.

Still, he made a strong impression on Ezra, the guy behind the counter at the dog place.

"Cool!" He came out from behind the counter when we walked into the store. "Is he a wolf? Where did you get him?"

"I think he's some kind of husky." I said. "He just showed up last night."

"Guess he needed you, huh?" Ezra winked at me, then proceded to fit the Hound out with every kind of collar, leash, harness, food bowl, water bowl, brush, flea comb, bed, and crate he thought we might need, plus generous supplies of kibble and treats. He even talked me into buying something called an elevated lounging platform, in case Deep Ellum dirt got too uncomfortably warm for a former Hell Hound.

We arranged for him to deliver it all the next day, then Ezra knelt before the Hound and carefully fitted his harness and collar.

"He's a gorgeous boy." Ezra ran his hands over the Hound's thick black fur. "But he's pretty skinny, and his coat almost looks like it's been burned in places. Poor guy. Do you think he was abused? He's so well behaved, though. Do you think he was somebody's pet? Maybe the owner is looking for him. I haven't seen any posters or notices online."

"I'll check around," I promised, although I was absolutely certain the Hound's former owner knew exactly where to find him. "I expect he's been lost for a while."

"What's his name?"

That stumped me. "Dunno. He hasn't told me yet." I looked at the Hound. He gazed back at me, as if he thought I was the most wonderful thing in the whole wide world. "Nutzo doesn't seem like a very good dog name, does it, Ace?"

The Hound wagged his tail at the word "Ace."

"Ace is a great name for him." Ezra ruffled the Hound's ears. "Do you like that name, Ace?"

The Hound woofed at Ezra, and then I swear he nodded at me. "Ace it is, then."

"Better than Deuce." Ezra stood up. "Deuce means two, and this guy would never be second in a pack."

Huh. Deuce was also sometimes used as a euphemism for the devil, and I guess the Hound had won out over that part of the hand he'd been dealt. "I think you're right. C'mon, Ace. Let's go home."

"And, hey, once he gets healthy, and all his fur grows in, you might want to save it. You know, when he starts shedding in the spring?" Ezra looked like a man who was trying to seem casual while really caring a lot about his point. "I have a friend. Callista. She spins dog hair into yarn for sweaters and stuff. I'll bet Ace here could give her some powerful fibers to work with."

Who knew? "I'll keep it in mind." I spent the walk home contemplating the nature of Ezra's friendship with Callista and the power she might find in yarn spun from Hell Hound fur.

I settled Ace into a warm, quiet corner where he could sleep without fear that his former pack mates might come back for him. Then I knew I had run out of excuses. It was time to deal with that damned fiddle. I'd thrown down a challenge to the fiddle's maker. Now I needed to figure out how to meet it.

I took the case back to my workbench and turned on my brightest lights. I had examined the fiddle pretty closely yesterday, so I set it aside, and made a more detailed survey of the case.

Under all the duct tape residue, it was a pretty basic case. The body was wooden, shaped to fit the fiddle and store the bow. It had originally been covered with black leather and lined with red velvet. Over the years, the velvet had gone bald. The leather had worn away on the corners and torn in a couple of places on the top and bottom of the case.

The duct tape had done the case no favors, but the latches

and hinges were completely useless—smashed, twisted, and well on the way to stripping the screws out of the wood. Curiously, the wood was still in pretty good shape, despite the scorch marks along the edges. The case could be fixed, but I wasn't sure it was worth it.

I flipped it open again, and turned my attention to the bow.

Like the fiddle, the bow appeared to be made of solid gold, although it was not nearly heavy enough to be actual gold. It was warm to the touch, and seemed to vibrate when I ran my fingers over it.

"You want me to play with you?" I asked it, unclipping it from the case and lifting it free.

In response, it all but flowed into my hand, weaving itself between my fingers until they were in the right position to hold it. It felt beautifully balanced. The vibration grew stronger, almost like a purr.

"Are you some kind of a cat?" I knew violin strings were not actually made of catgut, and bows were usually haired with horsehair, but who knew what might have gone into the making of this thing?

"Due diligence," I reminded myself. Best to get the basic tests out of the way, just in case I had missed something. But no, the golden bow did not scratch or melt, or behave in any way like real gold. Like the fiddle, it was probably made from a human soul.

But was it the same human soul? I narrowed my eyes at it. The vibration coming from the bow seemed completely different from the sense I got from the violin. But, once again, when I held the bow close to the fiddle strings, I felt an almost magnetic attraction between the two.

"I wonder . . ." I drummed my fingers on my workbench as I looked from fiddle to bow. Then I pulled the violin into the light and compared the two side by side. As the bow nestled next to the fiddle under the work lamp's glare, I could see what I had missed before. The bow was a slightly different color—a warmer, rosier gold—than the fiddle.

I set the fiddle aside once more. "So who are you?" I studied the bow more closely. "And why are you so happy to be here?" I sat up straight and held my hands out flat over the bow. "Let me see you," I commanded.

A shimmer of light ran the length of the bow and a change came over the hair. It still appeared to be gold, but its texture was different. No longer smooth and even, the bow hair now showed tight, close waves, as if someone had stretched extremely kinky hair as tightly as possible from one end of the bow to the other.

Something brushed against my leg, and I looked down to see Ace, newly awakened from his post-breakfast nap. Already his fur looked fuller and shinier, and I thought about Callista with her dog hair sweaters.

Which gave me an idea.

Abandoning the bow on the workbench, I chirped to Ace and headed for the shop's very large back room. It was where I stored all the odd but useful things I didn't have room for out front, and didn't want to throw away. I was pretty sure I had at least one spinning wheel back there somewhere. Ace helped me worm my way through decades of accumulated treasure until I located an old-fashioned, big-wheeled kind. It didn't have the foot pedals of more modern wheels, to keep the wheel moving while the spinner's hands worked the yarn. Still, I figured it would do.

I set it up by my workbench where the light was good, and looped the tensioning belts over the wheel. Then I pulled my chair close, and ran my fingers through my own hair, combing, tugging, adding a touch of juju until I had enough hair to make a small tail. I wound it onto the bobbin and fed it through the eyelet so there was enough to catch onto. Then I settled the bow on my lap and stroked my hand over the bow hair, down the whole length of it.

"Come on, now. Come on out of there," I murmured. As the first golden hairs came loose, I wound them into the tail of my own hair and set the wheel spinning. As they caught, I stroked the bow again, pulling more hair into the yarn, and watched as the bobbin began to take it up. Over and over I stroked the bow, and the golden thread began to fill the bobbin. Ace settled down to sleep at my feet. My hand flashed from bow to wheel and back again. The spokes of the wheel never slowed.

As the last of the bow hair twisted itself into the thread, thin strands of the golden bow itself began to peel off. Tid and Morsel crept in from the darkened shop to watch the whirling spokes. The bobbin grew fatter and fatter.

I don't know how long it took. Hours, at least. Possibly days. But in the end, the bow was gone, and there was nothing left but the smoothly gleaming golden thread that filled the bobbin from one end to the other.

I stood, stretching my arms up over my head and bending from side to side to work the kinks out of my back and shoulders. Ace, Tid, and Morsel followed my every move.

I looked at the cats, and back at the glittering thread. "I don't think I need your help for this next part," I said, and shooed all three animals out of the room.

Closing the door behind them, I turned back to the wheel. The end of the thread stuck out from the bobbin like a little tail, and I pulled on it, gathering more than a yard of the shining stuff into my hands. Then I flung it into the air and gave the wheel a strong push, spinning it back in the opposite direction.

"Let me see you!" I commanded.

The thread flew off of the bobbin, into the dark beyond the

reach of my workbench light. It pooled on the floor, piling up on itself, building, growing, taking a shape it hadn't held in who knew how long, until the wheel began to sing as it spun and the spokes flashed by so rapidly I knew the thread was pulling itself off the bobbin. As the last of the golden thread twirled away there was a flash, and the tiny tail of my own hair disappeared in a whiff of sulphur, taking the final traces of the bow-spell with it.

I heard a little hiccup, then a deeply indrawn breath. Something glittered and moved, back there in the darkness.

A woman stepped into my circle of light. She was tall and thin, with curves in all the right places and cheekbones high and sharp enough to etch glass. Her eyes were the same deep brown as her skin, and her dark, kinky hair fanned out around her head like a crown. She wore a gold-sequined evening gown, and a look of utter astonishment as she focused on my face.

"Miz Eddy?" she said.

Rosalie's Story

Chapter Five

"Rosalie?" I asked, dumbfounded. "Rosalie Wilson?"

"Oh, Miz Eddy! Am I ever happy to see you!" Rosalie flung herself across the workroom and wrapped her arms around me, hugging me as if her life depended on it.

Which it might yet. I tried not to get tangled up in her hair, and find a way to return her hug that didn't involve naked back or gaping cleavage. I settled for patting her on her bare shoulder.

She turned me loose at last, stepping back to give me a good, long look.

"Miz Eddy, you've changed." A frown flashed over her face. "Your clothes." She squinted into the light, toward the workbench and the spinning wheel. "I . . . I don't understand. It's been so long. How are you still here? How are you still you but . . . different?"

"Apparently you needed me."

That wouldn't make sense to her, of course.

"It's complicated. And not important right now. How long

have you been in that bow?" I looked her over from head to toe. I'd known Rosalie way back in the 1930s, when this place was a nightclub. She hadn't changed at all. In fact, I was pretty sure I remembered that dress. And if she hadn't changed, that meant...

"Wait a minute, Rosalie. Is that fiddle Henry?"

Tears welled in her big, brown eyes. "Oh, Miz Eddy, he didn't mean it. I know he didn't."

I pulled a second chair out from under my workbench and slumped into my own chair with a sigh. "Have a seat." I nodded her toward the second chair. "Tell it to me slowly. What did you get yourselves into?"

"Oh, Miz Eddy, I'm so ashamed." Rosalie sank onto the chair with the fluid grace of a dancer. She had been a bit of that, and a bit of a singer, and every inch a stunner, back when she and her husband, Henry Wilson, had a nightclub act together. "This mess is all my fault. I should never, ever, have paid any attention to that triflin' Robert Johnson."

Oh, for pity's sake. He might have been the greatest bluesman ever, but that man had brought nothing but trouble, jealousy, and strife to Deep Ellum. And Hell Hounds. Now it looked like he had a hand in the story of the golden fiddle, too.

"Tell me."

"It's just that Henry was in one of his moods, you know?"

I did know. Henry Wilson had been a handsome man, and a pretty fine fiddler, back when string bands were evolving into blues bands, and violins were more common than guitars. Rosalie was the one with all the warmth and charisma. She could light up a stage with her smile, but Henry was a serious musician, who was nearly as poker-faced onstage as those symphony guys. All his fire came from his unique style of playing. He could make that fiddle shout and moan better than any slide guitar guy, and sing prettier than Rosalie.

"He got to brooding and wouldn't talk to anybody. There wasn't a thing I could do to get him to tell me what was wrong." Rosalie's eyes grew wide at her remembered distress. "Not a thing! And then that Robert Johnson came in one night and started flirtin' with me like the men always do. I thought maybe, if I made my Henry a little jealous, I could get him to talk to me. So I let that Robert Johnson come on, and the next thing I knew my Henry had stormed out to the alley and was talking to that Nicky guy who used to hang around all the time. You remember him?"

I did. We'd known each other, off and on, for a long time. I figured we were about to reacquaint ourselves.

"My Henry was yellin' and stormin' and stompin' all around. Talkin' about those guitar players and how nobody wanted to hear his fiddle no more and how he wanted the whole world to beg to hear him." Rosalie shook her head, her eyes focused on the past.

"I knew we weren't getting booked as much, but I had no idea that's what he was upset about. My Henry is the best blues fiddler in the world! Everybody wants to hear him. That Robert Johnson was just a novelty, you know? Just the new guy in town. Before you knew it, he'd move on, but my Henry would still be there, and the people would still love him just as much as I did."

I figured this wasn't the time to tell her that Robert Johnson was now the king of the blues, and nobody except a few musicologists even remembered blues fiddlers like Henry.

"But then that Nicky guy said he could fix it, if my Henry would pay him what he asked." The horror grew in Rosalie's voice and face. "And Henry said he'd give his soul to have people beggin' to hear him like they used to do.

"Miz Eddy, that was just wrong of him." Her eyes met mine in a plea for understanding. "I never was much for church, but even I knew that was wrong. So I jumped in there, and tried to stop him. Tell him he was wrong, and people still wanted to hear him. Of course they did!

"And then that Nicky guy asked me if I wanted to stick with Henry or go off with Robert Johnson." She all but spat the name.

"I just laughed at him. I told him Henry was my man, and I loved him, and there was nothin' ever that would tear us apart."

"So what did he do?"

"Well, I didn't see exactly." Rosalie looked as hurt and puzzled as a child. "But the next thing I knew, Henry had turned into that awful golden fiddle, and I was lyin' there beside him like his bow. We could only touch when he was makin' music, and he only ever made the music he wanted to make when that Nicky guy was tempting some new sap with that fiddle."

She shuddered. "It was horrible. All those nasty, greedy people, grabbin' onto us, lustin' after us, only we was just a fiddle and a bow. Who lusts after that? And then, as soon as they got us, they'd start to fall all apart, and Henry would stop making music for them because he didn't want them to be better than him."

Rosalie leaned forward, clasping her hands. "I prayed so hard, Miz Eddy. I did. I prayed to God to deliver us and to Jesus to save us, but they never did nothin' and after a while I just thought, 'Miz Eddy would know what to do. Miz Eddy would save us.'"

She hung her head, her crown of hair falling forward to hide the shame in her face. "I know it was wrong, Miz Eddy, but after a while I just prayed to you. 'Save us, Miz Eddy. Save us.' That's what I said to myself every day, over and over. All day long."

And there it was. The reason that damned fiddle kept

coming back to my shop was that Rosalie Wilson had been praying for my help.

She raised her head and her eyes met mine again. I saw wonder, and hope, and a little fear in her heart, which is I guess what most folks feel when they're starting to think they're in the middle of a miracle but don't quite believe it. "And here you are. Can you save us, Miz Eddy?"

"Do you believe I can?"

I have to give her credit. She took the time to look me over good and do a more thorough observation of the workroom. The answer she gave me was true.

"I believe you are the only one who even wants to try, Miz Eddy."

Tears sprang into her eyes and glimmered there, not quite falling.

"What else do you believe in, Rosalie?" I tried to keep my voice gentle. "Tell me."

"I believe in Jesus Christ, our Lord and Savior, the way my mamma taught me to." Her voice quavered just a little. "But I don't think he believes in me."

"You'll have to take that up with him separately, once we get this current mess straightened out," I said. "You might be surprised."

"I believe in Henry." There was defiance in her voice now. "He's the best man I ever met and the best fiddler, too. I believe our love can conquer all." Her eyes shone with a fierce inner fire. "And I do believe in you, Miz Eddy. I do believe, if you got me this far, you can undo this whole horrible thing, and give my Henry back to me."

"Good enough." I nodded and stood up. "Consider yourself saved."

"What . . . You mean . . . That's it?" She struggled to her feet as she grappled with the new idea.

"Do you feel saved?"

She stopped to take stock. "I feel . . . hope, and I didn't have that before. I feel gratitude to you for helping me, and love for my Henry, that we still need to help." Her spine straightened as the idea of salvation took hold. "And I feel brave enough give that Nicky guy a piece of my mind, if he still happens to be around."

"There you go." I smiled as I watched the weight lift off her heart. "Salvation doesn't always come with light from above and a heavenly choir. You asked for it. You got it." I jerked my head toward the door out to the garden. "Now come on. We've got work to do."

Midnight

Chapter Six

It was near about midnight when the limo pulled up to my back gate. Not that I pay too much attention to time, but Nick is a real stickler for stuff like that. Image is everything to him.

So I have no doubt it was the actual stroke of midnight when the limo driver stepped out and opened the back door of that long black Caddy for his passenger.

The last time I'd seen Nick, he was a gambler, rooking people who would bet a whole week's wages on a roll of the dice. Black as his own withered soul, he'd been back then. These days he was passing for the kind of wealthy white developer who could talk folks into investing in condo towers like the one down the street. He always did have a way of knowing where his next opportunity lay.

He hustled himself out of that limo like a very busy man, who had better places to be and more important people to talk to. I doubted either was true.

I had left my back gate open, so I could see him pull up in the alley. He could see us, too. As I had with the Hell Hounds,

I'd set myself up next to my little patio table on the far side of the ornamental pool. The fiddle case lay open on top of the table, and Rosalie stood beside it, her hand on the violin's neck, her dress glittering in the light from the security lamp in the alley. Ace sat quietly beside me on the other side, ears up, eyes watchful. Tid and Morsel lurked somewhere in the shadows.

Nick's forward charge came to an abrupt halt when he reached my fence line. My gate might be open, but he could not cross my threshold without my permission.

He stood up a little straighter, and adjusted his red power tie, as if he'd meant to stop there all along.

"Evenin', Miz Eddy," he called to me.

"Nick."

"Fine night."

"Would be, if your big ass car wasn't spewing fumes into it."

Nick chuckled, as if we were sharing a little joke between friends. "Oh, well, now, Horace, you know, he likes to keep the heat on."

"I expect he does." I dipped my head in a nod. The limo's engine shut off.

Nick whipped around to look at the car, then turned back to me. "I see you're not in a hospitable mood."

"What do you want, Nick?"

"Nothing, really, Miz Eddy. Hate to bother you, even for a minute." He was all smiles and Southern charm. "It's just come to my attention you might have something that is mine."

"I don't believe that's true, Nick."

"I see it, sittin' right there on the table beside you." He nodded at the fiddle, then narrowed his eyes at Rosalie. "But what have you done with the bow?"

Rosalie shifted beside me, but held her ground. She only darted me the swiftest of glances before she raised her head to meet Nick's scrutiny.

"I saved her immortal soul, Nick. She's not yours anymore." No sense dancing around it. Our cards were on the table now.

Nick's carefully groomed eyebrows arched in polite surprise. "You? You saved her soul?"

"Tell him, Rosalie."

Rosalie stood up straight and tall, cleared her throat, and said what I'd told her to say, loud and proud enough for even Horace, in the soundproofed limo to hear her. "I believe in the Father, the Son, and the Holy Ghost. And I believe in Miz Eddy."

"Cute." Nick's focus shifted back to me.

"Times have changed, Nick. Used to be, when a man swore allegiance to his overlord, or a woman was sold into slavery, that bond held forever. But things are different now."

"Oh?" His voice was silken sarcasm.

"These days folks change their jobs, their political parties, even their religions all the time. It's called free will. Folks leave their old masters whenever they choose and pick new ones whenever they feel like it. Some never take masters at all."

"They only think they can do that." Nick sounded confident, but he crammed his hands into his elegantly cut suit pockets, and started to fiddle with whatever spare change or lint or damned souls he kept in there. "The fundamental rules haven't changed."

"Of course they have." I let myself laugh, mostly because I could see Rosalie was getting nervous. "People nowadays don't believe in your rules. They don't even believe in you. You're the punch line to an old joke, the loser in a catchy country song. And that makes you weak. Too weak to hold onto a soul that wants her freedom."

"Only God can redeem the damned." Nick took a fast step toward my threshold, and rocked back when he realized he still didn't have permission to cross.

"The thing is, Nick, the word 'god' is really more of a job description than an actual name. Even Old No-Vowels has a proper name. And the rule, as I understand it, is that, when a damned soul prays ardently, with her whole heart, for redemption, the god she prays to can redeem her."

I spread my hands as if the truth was obvious. "Rosalie Wilson prayed to me. I heard her prayer, and I have redeemed her."

"You!" Nick's contempt rippled all through that word. "You redeemed her? You are a god? You're nothing, Miz Eddy, and you'll be less than nothing the minute I have the police in your pathetic little pawn shop, searching for stolen property."

Rosalie whimpered beside me, and Ace rose to his feet, as Nick seemed to grow four feet in stature. Little flames burst from the pavement to lick around his shoes, and snap from his eyes and fingertips.

"Seriously, Nick? That's the best you can do? Ten feet tall, with some puny ground effects?" I shook my head. "My, oh, my. You're weaker than I thought."

"Stronger than you, you pathetic little worm," he snarled, squaring his shoulders and looking all masculine and menacing. His teeth became sharpened fangs, and his skin took on an unearthly green glow. Sulphur fumed the air around him.

"Is that what I am?" A light breeze danced from me to him, blowing his sulphur away. I let my own shell crumble. My spirit rose and spread. "Look at me, Nick. Is that what you see?"

Taller I grew, wider and deeper. All I was or ever had been, all that flowed from me, all the love and joy and belief that flowed into me blazed before him.

"Who am I, Nick?"

I topped the garden wall, then the shop itself, and burst out to spill down all the streets and splash up the sides of all the buildings. Over all the drunks and dilettantes, tattoo artists and hipsters, lovers and petty thieves. Over the squares yearning for adventure and the lost ones, yearning for the safety of a conventional life.

"Tell me who I am!"

I spread out over my beloved Deep Ellum until there was no mistaking my compass. I heard a ragged cheer go up from the folks on the street, not because they could see what Nick saw, but because they could feel it, deep in their souls, and they knew wonder when it came upon them.

And Nick, far below, gaped up at me in his own kind of wonder, until he caught himself, and his mouth snapped shut.

"Who am I, Nick?" I demanded. "What am I?"

"*Genius loci.*" I could have sworn there were tears in his eyes. "Well I'll be damned."

"More than likely. And what do your rules say about me and my kind?" I allowed myself to drift back down to something closer to human scale. No sense blowing everything on one special effect.

"A *genius loci* is the guardian god and spirit of a specific locale." He recited the answer as if this was some weird catechism. "Limited in geographical area, but within that area, all powerful."

"So I'll ask you again, Nick. Who am I?" I was only ten times his size now, so it wasn't hard to hear his answer, even though he mumbled.

"Miss Eddy Weekes, you are the *Genius Loci* and Spirit of Deep Ellum."

I figured that would do for now. No sense showing my whole hand. Girl has to have some secrets. I shrank back to my usual manifestation, still standing beside Rosalie behind the table.

Rosalie's eyes were wide as saucers. "I believe in the Father, Son, and Holy Ghost, and I believe in Miz Eddy," she recited.

"I-believe-in-the-Father-Son-and-Holy-Ghost-and-I-believe-in-Miz-Eddy. I believe in Miz Eddy. I do."

"Okay," Nick said from the gateway. He smoothed his neatly manicured hand over his five-hundred-dollar haircut. "The girl is yours."

"Kind of you to acknowledge the truth, Nick." I took Rosalie's hand in mine, patting fingers that felt half-frozen from fear, or awe, or whatever mix of the two she was feeling. What had she expected? She knew the rules, too.

"It's okay, sweetie," I said as her fingers clung to mine. "It's okay. You're free."

"Oh, thank you, Miz Eddy. I believe in you. I do. I promise I do. But what about Henry?"

Seven Deadly Sins

Chapter Seven

Nick's head snapped up at her words, and a satisfied little smile spread across his smoothly-barbered cheeks. "Yes, Miz Eddy. What about Henry?"

Rosalie snatched the golden fiddle out of its case and clutched it between her breasts. "Don't you touch him. Henry is mine."

"Henry has free will, same as anybody else," I said. "He will have to answer for himself. But come on in, Nick, now that you understand the ground rules." I eased up my boundary a little.

Nick moved forward with caution, stopping on the far side of the ornamental pool.

"But . . ." Rosalie turned her huge, sad, puzzled eyes to me. "How can he answer if he's still a violin? Change him back, Miz Eddy, like you did for me."

"That kind of work takes a while. Nick, here, might get bored."

"I can change him back." Nick smirked at Rosalie from

across the pool. "In far less time than it will take Miz Eddy to spin him out."

Rosalie eyed him warily. "You would do that?"

"I'd be happy to." Nick sounded all suave and generous. "If you think your love is strong enough to hold him."

In that instant, Henry changed from a golden fiddle to a long golden python. The snake wrapped itself around Rosalie, twining its tail around her legs and its head around her neck.

"I don't care what you look like! I love you!" Rosalie wrapped her arms tight around the snake. "My Henry gives the best hugs in the world." Her hand stroked the snake the length of its back, pressing it more closely to her body.

The snake morphed into an ink-black panther, roaring defiance an inch from Rosalie's nose. She buried her face in the fur of his neck and held on. "Oh, honey, you know I love a man with thick black hair," she purred.

The panther whirled away into the form of a young mesquite tree. Its inch-long thorns cut into Rosalie's flesh as storm winds tossed it back and forth.

"You always were a prickly bastard," Rosalie yelled, never loosening so much as a finger. "But I know how to keep that temper in trim."

Next came a column of thick, ropy lava that seared Rosalie's skin and sizzled her hair. "Oh, baby, I've missed your heat," she crooned, and lava changed into iron, cold enough to give her frostbite.

"So hard. My Henry's so hard."

The changes kept coming. Rosalie's wounds faded with each change, even as her responses became increasingly erotic. I figured Nick kept trying new shapes merely for the sick fascination of seeing how Rosalie would make love to each one.

When he got to the bear, she simply grabbed it by the balls.

"That's enough, honey," she said. The bear stopped struggling.

Nick gave a little snort of disgust.

Then, ever so slowly, the bear began to shrivel and stretch, morphing into a tall Black man in a blue pinstripe suit. He had a handsome face and hands that dwarfed Rosalie's delicate shoulders where he gripped them.

"Get your ugly hands off me, woman!" He tried to push her away but his movements were stiff and awkward, as if he had almost forgotten how.

"Shut the fuck up and come out of there, you stupid son of a bitch!" Rosalie's voice held all the power and authority of a wife who had loved her man so long and so deeply that she knew every button he had and exactly how to push each one.

"I am the best thing that ever happened to you, and you told me that yourself. So stop being such a goddamned stubborn fool!" Rosalie's scarlet fingernails dug into Henry's back as she rose to her tiptoes, grinding her hips against Henry's with all the pent-up lust of their decades as bow and fiddle. "And come home to Sweet Mama," she murmured into his ear, her voice dropping to a throaty growl.

Henry froze in place, one hand resting on her breast, the other cupping her ass.

Rosalie's lips moved over his cheek and down to his mouth. She kissed him. Hard. I'm pretty sure there was tongue.

Henry shivered, the tremor racing outward from his lips across his face and down the whole length of his body. Something barely visible peeled away from him, like a thin coating of ice, melting in the heat of the sun. His fingers flexed, and he pulled her closer, clutching her like a lifeline. "Rosalie?" he whispered.

"Oh, Henry!" She kissed him again, and this time he kissed back.

The storm of their passion blew up quickly. Each of them touched and stroked and groped the other as if there was nothing else in the world. If they ever found a place to lie down, the reunion sex was going to be spectacular.

"Oh, honey, I love you," Rosalie cooed.

"I'm sorry, baby, I'm so sorry," Henry whispered. "I'll do anything to make it up to you. Can you ever forgive me?"

"Of course I forgive you, Henry. Of course I do."

"This is disgusting," Nick glanced at the gaudy, golden watch on his wrist. "Can we move it along some?"

"True love make you queasy, Nick?" In point of fact, I thought we were right on schedule. I turned to the lovers.

"Just for the record, Henry, are you telling me that you have prayed ardently for forgiveness, and do you feel you have received it?"

"Oh, that's ridiculous." Nick spat into my ornamental pool. "He only prayed to her, not to you."

"You have to pray to Miz Eddy, Henry." Rosalie's tone was urgent. "Miz Eddy?"

Henry ripped is eyes off Rosalie's cleavage long enough to look around the garden. "Why? What is she doing here?"

"Let's take this one step at a time, shall we?" I decided to grab control before Nick could mess things up again. "Henry Jefferson Wilson, do you want to remain in the form of a golden violin, condemned for all time to seduce other poor saps into trying to make beautiful music on you, whilst being separated from Rosalie except when you're being played?"

"No!" Henry turned to face me, but held Rosalie even closer, if that was possible. "That was hell! I never want to go back to being that fiddle."

"And when you were in your deepest levels of despair, who did you think would save you? Who or what do you believe in?"

"I knew all along my Rosalie's love was the only thing that

could save me. She is always there when I need her. She will never desert me." Henry turned back to gaze upon Rosalie's beautiful, tearstained cheeks. "Even though I don't deserve her and never will."

"Miz Eddy," Rosalie whispered to him. "Baby, you have to pray to Miz Eddy, too, or it won't work."

"Not necessarily," I said.

"But Miz Eddy, he can't pray to me!" Rosalie's heartbroken eyes pleaded with me. "I can't save him! I'm no kind of a goddess!"

"Sometimes one believer is all it takes."

But just for the sake of due diligence, I turned back to Henry. "Tell me, Henry Wilson, do you feel saved? Is your soul in a state of grace?"

"My soul is always in a state of grace." Conviction rang in Henry's voice. "So long as I know my Rosalie loves me."

"Good enough for me," I told Rosalie. "If you forgive him, he's saved."

"The hell he is!" Nick lurched forward.

I widened and deepened the ornamental pool, even as he tried to leap across it.

Nick hung in midair a moment, as if he thought he could recalculate his trajectory. And in that moment, a sleek body broke the surface of the water, flinging itself directly at Nick. Needle-sharp teeth, set into alligator-like jaws, tore through his elegant trouser leg and sank into muscle and bone. The creature, long and supple as a river otter, but smoothly hairless, flipped up and over, throwing Nick completely off balance, before it fell back into the water, dragging Nick down too. They both disappeared with a glitter of green and gold scales, and the whisk of a whale-fluked tail.

Rosalie and Henry stared at the water, frozen in place.

Their eyes rose to meet each other, then turned in unison to me.

"Don't stand there gaping," I said. "You two need to get out of here. Henry, I've left my best, non-enchanted fiddle and bow in a case on the counter. There's a suitcase by the door with clothing and money, and a driver out front, waiting to take you to a friend's place in Heller. When you get there, ask for Waylon. Tell him Eddy sent you. Now go on. Get going!"

Hand in hand, the two of them broke for the shop and didn't look back.

I waited until I heard the front door bang behind them. Then, with a sigh, I began to build up the floor of the ornamental pool again.

I took my time. After a bit the water started to roil and froth, and Nick's head rose just above the waves.

While he was still floundering and blowing, trying to clear his eyes, Ace stepped forward, hiked his hind leg, and shot a perfect stream of pee onto the little bald spot I could see on the top of Nick's head. The urine smelled of brimstone and disdain.

Nick sputtered and slapped at the air until he finally had to duck back underwater to escape.

Ace turned, kicked a little dirt, and strolled into my shop, followed by Morsel and Tid.

When Nick came up again, he was steaming, but I could see he had his temper more or less under control. "Any more humiliations you want to heap on me tonight, Miz Eddy?"

"Depends," I said. "Is there anybody else around my place you've pissed off?"

"Not. That. I'm. Aware. Of."

"All right, then." I stepped over the pool and reached down to help him out on the alley side.

"What was that thing?" he asked as he squeezed water out of his suit and tried to straighten his tie.

"These days they'd call him a mosasaur. I just call him Fred."

"A dinosaur?" Nick's voice rose with outrage. "You have a dinosaur in your fish pond? They're extinct!"

"He's a friend." I shrugged. "We go way back. He asked for my protection."

Nick shook his head, took a deep breath, and dried himself with a snap of his fingers. It took him another minute or so to sort out all his trouser creases and get his pocket square refolded.

I waited until he had nothing left to fiddle with. "Are we done?" I asked at last.

"Just . . . a couple of theological points we need to clear up," he said. His eyes went a little squinty, but he managed to look at me.

"Okay." I waited.

"First of all, Rosalie Wilson, a goddess? That's the most ridiculous thing I've ever heard."

"This isn't a church, Nick. It's a pawn shop. Anyone can redeem anything if she has the right ticket."

His eye roll would have made a fifteen-year-old girl proud.

"What else?" I asked, since it didn't seem like he was in much of a hurry to get to his real point.

"Well . . . You beat me. Fair and square. I can't deny it. So, are you . . ." Now he sounded like a resentful little kid. "Are you going to kick me out of Deep Ellum?"

Just for a moment I let my mind wander over my special, sacred patch of ground. I saw the girls, like Pomona, eager to find their new way in life, and the guys, like Perkins, just looking for a little shelter. I saw long-time business owners, like Violet, clinging to a traditional vibe, and the new guys, pinning their hopes on the micro-breweries and high-rise towers that signaled safety, security, and gentrification.

I tried to picture all of that without envy, greed, or lust. How long could Deep Ellum's restaurants and bars continue to thrive without gluttony, sloth, and anger? Where would any of them be without at least a little pride?

"Kick you out of Deep Ellum, Nick?" I shook my head. "The place just wouldn't feel like home."

-The End-

DEEP ELLUM BLUES
G.S. NORWOOD

Deep Ellum Blues – The Second Novelette

By G. S. Norwood

*In loving memory of
Randall "Mudcat" Young,
Friend, officemate, and all-around great guy.
You were gone far too soon.*

Mudcat

Chapter One

Waylon never texts.

In all the zillion years I have known Waylon Smith, only once have I known him to reach out first. People go to him, sure. They call, text, e-mail, drop by when they can. People ask him for help, for favors, for a break or a lift. He responds generously, but he never asks for help himself.

Except for that very first time I met him. He asked me for some information, and under the circumstances, I could hardly refuse. Some punks had murdered his wife and stolen the fancy wedding ring he'd made her. He wanted to know if it had passed through my pawn shop in the Deep Ellum neighborhood of Dallas. But he didn't ask me to help him find it, much less find it for him.

So when my phone buzzed, deep in my pocket, I was surprised to see a text from Waylon.

Clyde Randall

That's all it said.

No introduction. No explanation. Just two words I

assumed were somebody's name. I guessed, if I wanted to know more, I'd have to call Waylon, which was the more usual way he did business.

I wasn't in the mood.

Spring had crept into Deep Ellum while I was napping the winter away. Now the native plants along the sidewalks had burst into a tangle of green, waking the bees with the promise of warm weather and early honey. I wanted to go out, smell the breezes blowing up from the Gulf of Mexico, and bask in the pale sunlight. It might only be sixty degrees out there, but I could feel the seasons changing in my bones.

Forget the puffy coats and sensible boots of winter! I cast off my regular flannel and denim for a pretty bohemian skirt with fringe at the hem, a bright, low-cut blouse, and red lace-up ankle boots with heels that would never suit icy city sidewalks. Spring had come, at least for a day, and as the *genius loci* of Deep Ellum, I was thirsty for every drop of new life my little corner of the world could offer.

I whistled for Ace, my reformed Hell Hound, but he was stretched out in my back garden like a giant patch of soot on the sun-warmed bricks. My two black cats, Tidbit and Morsel, detached themselves from his shadow only long enough to move into a brighter patch of sunlight.

"I thought dogs were supposed to enjoy walks."

Ace flipped his tail up in a half wag, exactly once, and resettled a little farther to his right. He would move with the sun, but clearly that was all the effort he wanted to exert.

"Okay, lazy bones. Suit yourself."

I stepped over the dog and his feline companions, circled the pond where Fred, the mosasaur, was idling just under the surface, and emerged through my back gate into the awakening world.

Is "sashay" too strong a word? My skirt swung with my hips

as I strolled down the street, greeting old friends and smiling at the tourists. My part of Dallas was bursting with its own kind of growth. High rise apartment buildings shot seventeen stories above the vintage one- and two-story storefronts they were crowding out. Venerable industrial warehouses had fallen in favor of bland multi-level parking garages. There was a new excitement in the air as gentrification took hold, but underneath, I sensed a wash of regret as old businesses folded and long-time residents sought shelter from the flood of rising rents and stricter regulations.

If the newcomers remembered any of Deep Ellum's history, it was from the 1990s, when the grunge of the neighborhood had been part of the allure, rather than something to sanitize and sweep out of the way.

I remembered when Deep Ellum had not yet emerged from the shallow inland sea where Fred and I swam together as babies. The human impact here was less than a quick breath in and out again. Things had changed before, and they would change again. I meant to enjoy what was here now.

So yes, I sashayed down Elm Street, breathing fresh air and absorbing all the new scents and sounds. I shared my energy with the native plants, bedded in along the parking strips. We both stood a little taller and bloomed a little brighter as I passed by. I felt no urge to hurry, even pausing to scan the portable sign outside the Sons of Hermann Hall.

One of the names on the sign made me blink.

The Mudcat Randall Band. Apparently, they were playing in the Grand Ballroom tonight.

"Clyde Randall," I murmured, wishing Ace had come along so I wouldn't be so obvious about talking to myself. "Mudcat Randall."

For the past few decades Waylon had run a honky-tonk out in Heller, Texas. There was nothing he loved quite as much as discovering new talent and launching it out to the rest of the world.

What were the odds?

I swung open the wooden double doors and stuck my head inside.

"Gert? You there?" Gert was the latest retired lady of German origin to manage the front desk and answer the phones. "It's Eddy."

"Come on in!" Gert's voice boomed down the hall from the bar at the back, echoing off the wooden floor.

I went in, my boots making the old boards creak. The Sons of Hermann were German immigrants who had formed a fraternal lodge back in the 1890s. The Sons of Hermann Hall, intended to host their meetings and events, was built in 1911, which made it really old by Deep Ellum standards. Regular human habitation here only went back to 1873. Buildings dating to the 1940s were now considered too old to be useful— at least as far as the developers were concerned. Those buildings melted away in favor of the glass, steel, and concrete of the new high rises, but the old wooden frame of the Sons of Hermann Hall still hunched on its corner of Elm and Exchange, offering swing dance lessons, the oldest bar in Dallas, and venue rental for any band that wanted a place to play.

"What can I do for ya? Need a beer?"

"Not just now, thanks." I pulled up one of the fancy new wood-and-wrought-iron bar stools and watched Gert unpack a box she'd set on the floor behind the bar. Her completely unnatural golden blonde curls bounced over her shoulders as she pulled almost-empty bottles of liquor off the shelf along the wall and replaced them with new stock. Or new, recombined stock from yesterday's mostly-empty bottles. I didn't ask.

"Who is the Mudcat Randall Band?"

"Don't really know. New guys." Gert disappeared below the bar again, then popped back up with more liquor. "Supposed to load in around four, sound check at six." Again, she ducked and reappeared. "Came from out west somewhere. Said they'd played pretty regularly. Built up a following."

Down she went for one last load. When she came up, she paused to meet my eyes. Smiled. "Some place in Heller called Waylon's."

Bingo!

I smiled back.

"Any tickets left?"

Sons of Hermann

Chapter Two

Quite a few people were trailing up the two wooden staircases from the main floor to the Grand Hall at Sons of Hermann that night. I paused on the landing to breathe in the very human scent of old beer, warm bodies, and that faint underlying musk of old buildings.

The audience members who worked their way past me were a mix of all that is Deep Ellum. Purple hair, sleeve tattoos, and outrageous piercings mixed with earnest young hipsters who made more money in a year at their tech startups than some saw in a lifetime. It seemed everybody wanted to discover the next big thing. Maybe the Mudcat Randall Band was it.

But maybe not. I found a seat about halfway back from the corner stage and adjusted my folding chair to get a better view. The band's onstage gear looked pretty modest. A no-name beginner bass with an equally cheap amp stood to the left, while a lovingly used Squier Stratocaster shared a stand on the right with . . . I squinted at the acoustic guitar, trying to figure it out. Was that an old Stella? It had what looked like an after-market electric pick-up the player had probably installed himself. The Strat was attached to a respectable Fender Princeton tube amp that had been around many, many blocks at least twice. They wouldn't get much for any of it at my pawn shop, even if I was feeling generous.

The drum kit was a different story. Flashy red Pearls with Zildjian cymbals. I figured maybe a thousand dollars' worth of percussion equipment, with no evidence of the dings and nicks all instruments pick up during a life on the road.

Interesting. I wondered if Mudcat was the guitar player or the drummer. Not the bass player. He had an amateur's rig.

As the audience settled into their seats, Gert worked her way through the room, moving people over who had left single chairs empty on either side of themselves, guiding couples to the newly vacant pairs of chairs, and making sure everybody was happy. When they were, she strode up to the front of the stage, pulled a wireless mic out of her hip pocket, and blew into it as a test. Todd, the sound guy at the back of the room, gave her a thumbs up, and she cleared her throat.

"I want to thank you all for being here tonight," she said as the crowd got quiet. "These gentlemen—they call themselves the Mudcat Randall Band—are here for two nights to test out some new material before they head to Austin, so I want you to make them feel real welcome."

A ripple of applause ran through the crowd.

"And if you like them, I want you to tell your friends and come back tomorrow, so they'll have people to listen to them again. Okay? Thank you. Please welcome the Mudcat Randall Band!"

She switched off her mic and waved toward the corner, where three white guys in blue jeans, scruffy t-shirts, and authentically scuffed-up boots huddled together. They peeled apart at her signal and the first—a husky, dark-haired man with a scrub of a beard—took his seat behind the flashy trap set.

Next came a painfully skinny guy with limp ginger hair and a black leather vest over his ragged white t-shirt. The bass player. His rig might be for an amateur, but he was clearly trying to summon a rock star attitude of strut and superiority.

Last came the guitar player. He was taller than the other two, and his lean frame had filled out with adult male muscle. Long brown hair framed his rectangular face, with one tousled lock falling over his forehead to hide his eyes. Handsome, with high cheekbones and a firm, sharp chin, but when he finger-combed his hair back he looked much younger than I expected. He should have been smiling out of a high school yearbook, standing next to the Homecoming queen, rather than stepping onto a tiny stage in a musty rental hall above a bar.

He seemed a little shy in meeting the audience, although he steadied into a more confident stance the moment he picked up his guitar.

"Good evening." His voice was deep and calm with a trace of west Texas accent. "I want to thank you all for coming out tonight. I'm Mudcat Randall, and this is my band. That's Tim on bass."

Tim fiddled with his tuning, but didn't look up.

"And Tico on drums."

Tico hit a cliched ba-dump-dum and finished with a tap to one of his shiny cymbals.

"Tim and I have been playing together since we were babies, out in Heller, Texas, but Tico just joined us yesterday. We're going to play you some tunes and see if we can pull it all together in time to go down to Austin on Sunday. We're playing a showcase at South by Southwest next week, and we want to be ready. Can ya'll help us with that?"

The crowd applauded. A few of them whistled.

"All right then!" Mudcat ducked under his guitar strap and settled his Strat on his shoulder. "Let's get this party started!"

The band kicked off with a cover of Stevie Ray Vaughan's *Pride and Joy,* which seemed like a gutsy choice to me, seeing as how Stevie Ray was a Dallas native who had played every bar in town by the time he was of legal age to drink. They did a good job, though—better than good—and the audience fell right in with that distinctive blues shuffle, swaying along and giving a rousing round of applause when the song ended.

They moved on to *Key to the Highway*—more B. B. King than Little Walter—then segued into the other Kings: Freddy and Albert. By the time Mudcat worked his way around to Hound Dog Taylor I had begun to realize that he was a very good guitar player. He could cover just about any blues style, from Chicago to Mississippi, with energy and precision. He brought a freshness to each song, which reminded me of why they were hits in the first place. But, somehow, he wasn't making them his own.

He finished *Wild About You Baby* with a flourish, then brushed the hair out of his eyes once again and met the audience's applause with a smile so broad and genuine it lit up the whole room. The applause rose a notch or two, augmented by more than one "Yeah!"

"It's real special for me to be here tonight." He unbuttoned his strap and set the Strat aside, picking up the Stella instead. "Here in Deep Ellum, where all the greats have played." He scanned the room. "Maybe on this very stage. Blind Lemon Jefferson, T-Bone Walker, Robert Johnson. Robert Johnson recorded some of his most famous songs just a mile down the street from here. Did you know that?"

Of course they knew that, and whistled in response.

"This is sacred ground for blues players, kinda the way the Ryman Auditorium is sacred for country musicians. I can feel a special energy right here in this room that just shouts to me that I'm in Deep Ellum, following in those footsteps."

A special energy? He could feel that? I glanced to each side. Nobody else seemed to notice my presence or attach any significance to it. But when I looked back to the stage, I met his gaze straight on, and saw what I hadn't seen before. He had a kid's face, and a young man's body, but his eyes were old, and sad, wary, and wise far beyond his apparent years. It jolted me, that gaze, and I am rarely jolted.

No wonder Waylon wanted me to check him out.

He tuned up the Stella and launched into an energetic run of Deep Ellum classics: *Black Snake Moan, They Call it Stormy Monday,* and *Hell Hound on My Trail.* From there he switched back to the Strat and swung into more contemporary stuff, checking in on Buddy Guy's *Stone Crazy,* Keb' Mo's *City Boy,* and even taking a stab at Sonny Landreth's *Somebody's Gotta Make A Move.*

He nailed the lyrics, his rough-edged baritone capturing the song's desperation and regret. But when it came time for the solo break, something different happened. For once he didn't shoot for a note-by-note cover of the original. Instead, he hit a lick I hadn't heard him play before, took a run at a complex chord progression, and then sailed into a solo filled with tremolo, harmonics, and a lot of string bending.

I focused in to see what he was doing and realized there was something different about his hands. For one thing, they were huge, as if he was still a puppy who hadn't grown into his paws yet. And as those long, supple fingers flowed over the frets I saw a kind of golden haze, filled with a faint, occasional spark, as if he was striking flint against the strings, but not quite catching fire.

I have seen a lot of guitar players. I have never seen that.

The crowd, at least, was catching fire. As they began to

cheer, Mudcat closed his eyes and let the music lift him above the audience, the noise, the sweat, and the beer to a place where only the most fearless musicians ever get to go.

When he drew the song to a close, and brought us all back down to earth again, the crowd went wild. Cheering, whistling, stomping, and clapping. He swiped the hair out of his ice blue eyes and smiled as if he was just waking up from really great dream. The audience wanted encores. He obliged, his band-mates gamely pitching in to support him, although I could see they hadn't been touched by the same magic.

He thanked us all for listening. Urged everybody to come back tomorrow and bring friends. From the way half the audi-ence rushed the stage, I didn't think he'd have much trouble drawing a second crowd.

I held back, watching Tico and Tim, the drummer and the bass player, secure their instruments and wade through Mudcat's throng of admirers to step down off the stage. A slim blond man in a slick black suit shook their hands, clapped them on their backs, and drew them off to the side to talk.

The crowd around Mudcat began to thin until it was mostly young women, hoping to catch his attention. He smiled at each, thanked each for being there, and kept glancing up, looking around as if he expected to see somebody else. When his eyes landed on me his smile broadened into a full-on grin that flashed warmth and delight all around the hall.

"Hey there," he said, as if we already knew each other. "Good to see you here tonight."

"You sounded great." I stepped forward and the hopeful young women melted away. I extended my hand. "Eddy Weekes."

"Really? Waylon Smith told me to keep an eye out for you! Great to meet you." He reached for my hand, encumbered by the guitar. With a little growl he stepped back, ducked out from under his guitar strap, and settled the Strat gently back into the cradle of its stand. "So, you liked it?"

"It was good."

His eyes lit up and his grin flashed once more. I wondered what he saw, and what Waylon had told him about me.

"Hey, come meet the band." He tilted his head and I followed him toward the men in the corner.

"Guys this is Eddy Weekes." His hand hovered over my arm, guiding me toward them but not quite touching my skin. "Eddy, this is Tim, my best friend and forever bass player."

I nodded to the weedy kid with the lank red hair.

"And Tico, our new drummer."

"Tico," I murmured.

"And this is Mr. Ashton Beele. He wants to be our manager."

I turned to the man in the sharp suit and smiled.

"Hello, Nick," I said.

Mosasaur Games

Chapter Three

Nick's smile was suave, his eyes politely puzzled. "Have we met?"

I shrugged. "My mistake." Which was my way of telling him I wouldn't interfere. Nick, Old Scratch, Beelzebub, or whatever he was calling himself today, and I had operated side by side for a good long while, mostly by ignoring each other's existence.

I am a nature spirit, not a human deity, and I believe in free will. That is, I believe each individual human is free to make whatever hideous life-altering mistakes he or she chooses. It's none of my business. I'm not here to save any souls, unless somebody asks for my help.

Mudcat had pasted on a smile that said he hoped we could all get along. "Ashton booked us all rooms at the W."

"A suite for the after-party." Nick brushed it away as if it was nothing.

"The W." Expensive, flashy. The kind of place these country boys would read as big city class. Clear the other side of downtown Dallas from Deep Ellum.

"You should come." Nick's smile grew sharper. He knew full well I was rooted in my personal turf and could not leave it.

"Yeah! Please come!" Mudcat looked like a hopeful puppy.

"I'm sorry. I've already made plans for the evening." I really was sorry, but an invitation, even from the star attraction, wasn't a prayer for divine intervention.

"Don't worry, Mudcat." Tim clapped his old friend on the shoulder. "There'll be plenty of girls there. Ashton promised. So come on! It's time to party!"

Tico closed in on Mudcat's other side as Nick looked toward the door.

"Wait! My stuff!" Mudcat pulled away, turning back toward the stage.

Two large men in dark suits emerged from the shadows next to Nick. One bent to whisper in his ear. The other stared at me as if he thought that might intimidate me.

"Horace has the limo out front," Nick announced. "Come on, boys. Travis and Dando can load up your stuff, drive the van over to the hotel. We don't want to let the champagne get warm."

"Or the girls get cold." Tim was clearly looking forward to sampling some of Nick's party favors.

Mudcat looked from them to the stage, then back to me. "I..."

"It was a pleasure to meet you." I nodded to him, ignoring the rest. "I hope we have the chance to talk again sometime."

"Will you come tomorrow night?"

"Wouldn't miss it."

I'd be here. I wondered if he would.

Morning broke warm and cloudless. I had spent the night in my garden, watching the moon rise over Deep Ellum and thinking about all the trouble a young man like Mudcat could get into at one of Nick's parties.

"Free will, Eddy. He's a grown man," I repeated for the umpteenth time. "I don't know what Waylon sees in him anyway."

But I did. There was something different about young Mr. Mudcat. Clearly Waylon had seen it during the many times Mudcat Randall had played Waylon's club. I had glimpsed it in flickers of gold as his fingers danced over his guitar strings. And Nick damn sure saw it, or else why was he so eager to get Mudcat under contract?

It certainly wasn't Tim he was after. And I would almost swear Tico belonged to Nick already.

I knew what he was trying to do. He'd paint a beautiful picture, filled with girls, glamor, and glory, then offer the boys his standard "Rich and Famous" contract.

He'd keep his end of the bargain, too. At least for a while. Mudcat Randall would ascend to the musical heights, become wealthy and adored, be hailed as a star. But addictions would follow, and disease. He would struggle with demons, real or imagined, and be dead well before he hit forty, meeting his end in some gruesomely painful way.

I knew the story. I'd seen it far too many times.

"Well, it's his if he wants it."

I rose from my chaise. The sun peeked over the eastern wall of my garden, and Fred stirred in the depths of his pool. I felt the new season rustling and whispering all around me, and I wanted to move.

With a flick of my fingers Fred's pool opened wide. My clothing began to melt away as my foot dipped into the water.

Then my human shape shifted entirely until I sank into the warm, salty sea of long ago, a mosasaur like Fred.

Fred's pool is not really a pool. It's more like a pocket of time and space, created for him when he asked me to protect him from a meteor and climate change far more abrupt and drastic than anything humans worry about today. Beneath the surface of his pool lies a whole ecosystem lifted from the warm, shallow waters of what geologists call the Western Interior Seaway. Fred calls it home.

I call it a decorative garden accent.

And sometimes, an excellent swimming hole.

Fred rose to greet me, delighted by the chance to race a playmate he didn't get to match wits with too often. We surged through the water, diving and leaping, spinning and looping, twining around each other in a game as old as spring itself, then breaking apart again to snatch at the little fish that shared his sea.

I felt my spirit shake off all human constraints, stretch, and relax, spread out in every direction, until I became one with the earth, the water, and all that was in it.

Hours and days are not worth tracking in Fred's pool, so I have no idea how long I was there. I only knew the joy of being and the freedom of frolic and fun.

Until . . .

Something nagged at me. Something from the world outside.

I pulled my energy back into focus and felt the tug of someone needing me to be there.

Fred and I floated up to the surface of the pool, happy, tired, sated. The tug came again, with more urgency than before.

"All right, already. Can't a girl get a little . . ."

Well, apparently not. The tug became a constant throb—the heartbeat of a desperate creature.

I found my feet, and then the shallow bottom. Rising out of the pool, I shed my mosasaur form with the water that poured off me and assumed my human aspect as I returned to dry land. Dry hair and dry clothing, too.

"Hold your horses. I'm coming." I closed Fred's pool back down to its normal size. Ace, Tid, and Morsel rose from their naps to trail after me as I moved from the sunlit garden to the dark of the not-yet-open pawn shop. I flicked on the overhead lights, and saw a shadowy human form lurking outside the front door.

The throb became a flutter of hope as I flipped my sign from "Closed" to "Open" and unlocked the door.

"Mis Eddy? This is your place? I didn't know . . ."

"Hey there, Mudcat." I opened the door just enough to speak to him face to face. He looked pale, exhausted, and more than a little frantic.

"What's going on?"

"I need . . . I lost . . ." He took a deep breath. "I was looking for a pawn shop. I didn't know I'd find you. But Waylon told me to ask for you if I ever . . ." He looked up and down the street, as if expecting an attack. "I need help. Can you help me?"

I swung the door open a little wider. "Come on in."

He took a shaky step forward and crossed my threshold.

Double Vision

Chapter Four

"It's alright. Whatever it is. We can fix it." I eased him further into the shop and closed the door behind him. Flipped the sign back to "Closed."

The shop, which exists in its own pocket of time and space, effectively disappeared from the street unless somebody else turned up, needing my help.

Mudcat stood where I'd left him, staring around.

Okay, it's not the prettiest pawn shop in the world. I will admit that I have done little in the way of modern design or marketing displays. It's a jumble of jewelry cases and musical instruments, small appliances, furniture, and camping gear. A ton of baby stuff, plus a few firearms. The layout doesn't make a lot of sense, but nobody comes in to browse, and I know where everything is. More or less.

"This is . . ." Mudcat did a slow pan of the whole sales floor. "This is amazing!"

"Have you had your coffee yet this morning?"

"What?" He turned back to me. "Coffee? No. You have coffee?"

"I'll tell you what." I eased around so I was between him and the garden. "Let's go back there and talk for a minute. I'll bring you coffee, and you can tell me what you need me to help you with, okay?"

I took a step toward the garden and he followed like a zombie, gawking at everything he passed.

"And you can meet my crew." Tid and Morsel hopped up onto the sales counter as we approached.

"You have shop cats!" Delight spread across Mudcat's face. "Hey, kitties, how ya doin'?"

Tidbit reserved her judgement, but Morsel, always a whore for affection, stepped up to butt his head into Mudcat's outstretched hand.

Ace surged out of the darkness in the back hall, blocking the way to the garden.

"I have a dog, too."

"Whoa! A really big dog!"

Ace stared at him, but did not bark or growl.

"Is he friendly?"

"It depends." Largely it depended on who a person consorted with. Nick's buddies did not get a warm reception from my former Hell Hound.

But, as he stepped forward to sniff over Mudcat's blue jeans, Ace's tail began to swish slowly back and forth. Which answered one question for me. Mudcat hadn't signed any contracts yet.

"I think he likes me!"

"Seems to." I nodded toward the door into the garden. "Go on back and find a seat. I'll bring the coffee."

I made an extra chaise next to Fred's pool in the time it took Mudcat to reach the garden door, then pulled a mug from the storage room and fresh French Roast coffee from the restaurant down the street.

"You take milk or sugar?" I called out to Mudcat.

"Black is fine."

I got a couple of biscuits and small bowls of butter and honey, just in case he found his appetite. I wasn't sure he'd have the stomach yet for eggs or sausage.

He was standing by his chaise, looking around the garden, a smile spread over his face.

"This is some place!" He turned to take the coffee tray from me and set it on the little table between his chaise and mine. "Who knew there'd be a garden like this in the middle of the city? This is great. Only one mug?"

I held up my hand. "I've already had my jolt for the morning." I waved at his chaise. "Sit down. Take a breath. Tell me what's going on."

He more or less collapsed onto the chaise, grabbed his mug of coffee and took a deep swallow. Then he sighed, and I watched his shoulders slump down a full two inches from where they'd been hunched up around his ears.

"How was the party? Did you get any sleep last night?" I settled onto my own chaise, realizing only then that I seemed to have clothed myself in tight denim leggings and a bright, flowing tunic. I kicked off concho-studded flip-flops and swung my feet up.

"God! The party was so weird." Mudcat sat on the edge of his chaise, facing me. "I mean, you come offstage and you're jacked, right? All that energy from the audience. And we were in Deep Ellum. Do you know how many years I've dreamed of playing here? So I was really bouncing off the walls, but when we got to the hotel suite . . ." He frowned into his mug. "It was just . . ."

He puffed out a breath. "I don't even know what planet those women were from. They were all sleek and stylish and perfectly groomed, but all they wanted was . . . was to "party," and I wasn't sure if they wanted the booze or the food or me. It was all just candy to them. I felt . . . They didn't even see me. Had no idea who I was. They just knew I was "the star." Like that meant something. I'm not a star. Were they hookers? Had Ashton paid them to be like that? I don't know, but it was all fake. They were all over me, but I just wanted to talk to somebody."

He sighed again. "I wish you could have been there."

"How did Tim like it? And Tico?"

"Tim was in country boy heaven. He couldn't get enough. Went straight from beer to Jack, with a girl on either side of him. I've never seen him act like that. I was embarrassed for him. And Tico . . . I don't know about Tico. He disappeared into the other room. The room with the—" He broke off and looked at me guiltily.

"The room with the drugs."

"I figured. I didn't go back there. Tim keeps teasing me about it. Says I'm the whitest white boy there is, but that stuff just messes with my playing. I've got enough trouble finding C, F, and G, without making my fingers clumsy on purpose."

"You do not have any trouble finding C, F, and G."

He hid a little smile behind his coffee mug as he took another sip.

"So what happened?"

"Oh, well, eventually those two guys who work for Ashton got back with our gear. They headed for the back room with Tico. Ashton and Tim disappeared with all four girls. I just wanted some quiet time to wind down and process everything, you know?"

I nodded.

"So I went down to the parking lot to get my guitar out of the trailer. Only the trailer was open and all our stuff was gone!"

"Stolen?"

"Somebody had ripped the door right off the hinges. I thought for sure the hotel security camera would have seen something, but I guess it wasn't working because it was all just blur and static."

"You don't have anything?"

"I don't know what they would have wanted with it. Most of it was so old it wasn't worth a dime. But we have a gig tonight, and South By next week in Austin." He gripped his mug and frowned down into Fred's pool as if he was seeing the future as a bottomless abyss.

"Why did you come here?"

He flopped back onto his chaise with a sigh. "I don't even know. I thought maybe the thieves would have pawned our stuff, and Deep Ellum was the place for pawn shops. Only there really aren't any here, are there? Except this place. And then I remembered Waylon told me that, if I ever needed any help, to find you, so I just started . . . praying, I guess." He ducked his head, shading his eyes behind those long, floppy bangs. "I know that sounds dumb. And really country. Do city folks even believe in praying?"

"Some of them."

"Well I prayed. That I'd find you. And you could help."

"So you did. And I can." I lifted his empty mug from his hand. "Refill?"

He shook his head.

"Try a biscuit. It's local honey."

He laughed, shook his head. Picked up the biscuit anyway.

"I'm surprised Ashton didn't offer to help."

"Oh, he did." The biscuit crumbled away in his fingers. Ace, who had been lurking behind the table, inched forward to lick the crumbs up as they fell.

"He told us to forget about all that ratty old stuff. He'd give us an advance, help us buy all new. Shit, Tico's rig was practically new already, and Tim couldn't wait to spend money he doesn't have on the rig of his dreams."

"But you came here?"

"I just . . . okay, you're going to think I'm crazy."

"Maybe. Tell me anyway."

He bit into his lower lip for a moment, thinking. "Do you ever . . . do you ever feel like you're seeing—I don't know—like you're seeing two levels of reality at the same time? Like you're seeing what's in front of you, but then also something really different underneath it?"

"Do you?"

"Sometimes. It's weird. Anyway, I just . . . I don't want to be beholden to Ashton like that. I mean, he's been good to us and all, and I know he wants to sign us to his artist management roster, but I don't want him buying my rig. I've heard about deals like that, you know? It's easy to take a loan against future earnings, but then there are no earnings, now or ever, and you owe a whole pile of money to some guy who can't manage your band out of a paper bag and . . . I don't know. I guess I want to pay my own way. That's something I learned from my dad."

"Your dad the independent type?"

"My dad's the type who attaches ugly, sticky strings to everything he offers. It's never done from love, only to leverage a better bargaining position."

He sounded beyond bitter.

"I guess you and your dad don't get along."

"You'd guess right. I broke all ties to him when my mom got cancer and he dumped her for a younger woman. One like those girls at the party last night."

I wondered if Nick had misjudged his mark. It wasn't like him, but there's a first time for everything.

"No drugs, no girls, no fancy guitars. Are you sure you're cut out for the life of a rock star?"

"Onstage is the only time I ever feel completely real," he said, his blue eyes meeting my green. "When my fingers are flying, and the song is true? The people are really into it, and the energy we share is a spiritual experience? I'd sell my soul for a lifetime of that."

Finding C, F, and G
Chapter Five

"Well, okay, then." I sat up and looked at the tray. The mug was empty and both biscuits had disappeared somewhere. I hadn't seen him eat a bite, so I guess Ace got all the crumbs.

I swung my feet down to the ground and stood up. Mudcat moved to stand up too, but I waved him back. "Tell me about the gear you need. Do you have preferences? Fender? Gibson? Paul Reed Smith?"

"I . . . You know, it's weird. Fender is the guitar, right? If you're playing electric, I mean. A good Strat can do just about anything, stand up to all the stress of the road, and if it does break, you can get parts for it in any city. So that's a no brainer."

"You had a Squier?"

"A starter Strat, yeah. All I could afford."

"And the Stella?"

"Found that at an estate sale and put the pickup in myself. It had a solid wood top, but it still might be nice to upgrade to something with a bigger voice.

"Lot of blues history made on a Stella."

"Yeah." He looked down at his boots. When he looked up again his focus slid off to someplace over my shoulder. "It's not really the brand, so much, as the feel." He squinted at me as if he was looking into the sunrise. "You're gonna think I'm weird."

"You keep saying that, but you haven't come up with anything weird yet."

There was that grin again—the one that could light up a room, and make most women forgive him all his trespasses.

"It's like . . . it's like the instrument has a soul."

Not weird. I could tell him stories.

"Or maybe it just absorbs the energy of the person who plays it." He tilted his head to the left, shrugged. "Anyway, when I play a guitar, I like to listen to its story, see if I can get a feel for where it's been. The ones that feel like we could be friends? Those are the ones I buy."

"Then let's see if we can find you some new friends." I held up my hand to keep him in his seat. "You stay put. I'll bring the instruments. Do you have a price range?"

"Well . . ." He named a couple of figures, which were actually higher than I'd guessed he could go, and certainly something I could work with.

"That's doable," I said. "One more thing. Do you trust me?"

I saw a little flicker of fear in his eyes, but he nodded.

I reached into my back pocket, where I found a sleep mask, which I tossed to him.

"A blindfold?" He frowned at it.

"You wear that. I'll bring you guitars. We'll see what they tell you, okay? Put that on and all you'll know is how they feel. You won't waste time trying to figure out how much they'll cost you. I promise I won't break your budget."

I also didn't want to physically lug a lot of guitars and amps out of storage, which I would have to do if he could see me.

"Count to fifty," I told him. "I'll be back."

I started with five of the better Fender Stratocasters and a couple of Telecasters I had in the back. No need to bother him with the ragged-out guitars that would need a lot of repair, no matter how classic they might be or what their history was. He needed a guitar he could play tonight.

He was going to need an amp, too, so I pulled out one that was slightly better than his old Princeton, but still not super high-end. By the time I got everything back to the garden, he was up and pacing around, mask in place, somehow neatly avoiding Fred's pool. Ace, Tid, and Morsel sat on the sidelines, watching him like spectators at a tennis match.

"This blindfold thing is kinda cool," he said. "I get a whole different sense of the space. It seems . . . bigger, somehow."

"Try this." I handed him the first guitar and plugged it into the amp. His perception of my space intrigued me. Maybe it was related to that thing he'd mentioned about seeing different levels of reality.

Once the guitar was in his hands, he clearly stopped wondering about my garden. All his focus went to the instrument he held. His fingers danced up the strings, he made a couple of adjustments, and began to play.

Then stopped abruptly.

"Whoa." He handed the guitar back to me. "That was one messed up dude."

Yes. He had been.

"Sorry. I mean, it's a nice guitar and all but ..."

"Not friendly."

"Not even a little. Nice amp, though." He began fiddling with the next guitar while he considered it. "Not a Princeton. Deluxe Reverb?"

"Yes."

"Gonna be a reissue if it's in my price range. Blackface or silver?"

"It's actually a tweed."

"No kidding? Very cool."

All of which was guitar speak for "you probably don't need to bring out any more amps."

Mudcat worked his way through the guitars, one by one, offering shrewd assessments of their former players along the way. When I handed him a tobacco burst Strat from the late 1980s, he bounced it a little, testing its balance before settling the strap on his shoulder.

"Feels nice." His fingers flickered up the rosewood fretboard, shredding a little chromatic scale. "This thing hasn't been played much at all." He hit a couple of power chords, and his face broke into that killer smile. "But she wants to be."

He ran through the opening riffs of nearly all his setlist before settling into the steady shuffle of *Pride and Joy*, which he played clear through, including a solo that was not Stevie Ray Vaughan's. His whole body rocked with the rhythm of the music. The longer he played the further the other guitars, my garden, and the whole world receded from his awareness until I could tell it was just him and this particular instrument, locked together in a duet that was almost sexual.

It took him a minute to come back to earth when he was done.

"Yeah. Wow." He nodded as he pulled his focus back to the practical. "Sweet. Who would pawn a guitar like this?"

"A man who had other guitars and wanted something else more urgently. He was broke at the time." I stood up from my chaise. "So that takes care of the amp and the Strat?"

His face split into that wide, wild smile that said he'd glimpsed the gates of heaven. "I can afford both?"

"They've been in the back for a while. We're not at your price limit yet."

"All right then!" He pushed the blindfold up onto his forehead and looked at the Strat he was still holding as if he was looking at the face of the woman he would marry. "Jesus, she's beautiful!"

"I hope you'll be very happy together. Now, about your Stella."

He turned back to me but held onto the Strat. "Okay."

"Look, this place has been here for a long time and I have a zillion old Stellas, Harmonies, Kays . . . You name it, I probably have it. Some of them date back to T-Bone Walker's time." At least one of them dated back to T-Bone Walker himself, but I wasn't going to take Mudcat there. "You want vintage, I can find you something."

He blinked, clearly thinking. Turning away from me, he carefully settled the Strat back onto the only empty guitar stand left beside the amp. His gaze moved to the other guitars. "Wow. This is some prime stuff." His fingers gave the Strat one last caress before he fastened the closure on the stand.

"Don't look at them. You know you don't want any of them. You'll just get distracted by their paint jobs. What function did the Stella serve for you? Did you ever wish you could play something else?"

His eyes were so damn blue, and a little haunted. "I loved that old Stella but . . . Do you have any resonators?"

"Put the blindfold back on."

It didn't take us long to find him a cheerful mahogany Gretsch resonator guitar, and then a sweet little grand concert style acoustic from Taylor.

"Man, Waylon wasn't kidding when he said you could help me." Shedding the blindfold, Mudcat studied the three guitars he had selected with some degree of amazement. "I can't believe my new after-hours pickin' guitar is a solid koa Taylor."

"It's not like I handed you a pre-war Martin." Since his

blindfold was gone, I was actually, physically, picking up guitars to carry back to storage.

"Oh, here, let me help." He moved to put the Taylor down, but I waved him off.

"Sorry, hon. Nobody goes into the back room but me. Too much stuff back there. You'd never come out again. Just give me some music to schlep by."

He settled back onto his chaise with the Taylor in his hand and began to finger pick basic arpeggios to a shuffle beat while I moved the first of his rejects into the hall between the garden and the sales floor. Ace took up a position at the garden door to keep Mudcat from sneaking a peek while I poofed stuff from the hall back into storage.

Ace needn't have bothered. Once he had my permission to play, Mudcat's focus was all on the guitar. The arpeggios quickly became a melody, and the melody soon spiraled into a theme with variations.

As I slapped the last of the guitar dust off my leggings, I listened, analyzing.

The music didn't sound like anything I'd ever heard before; a blend of country rock with traditional blues that wasn't Stevie Ray, or Derek Trucks, or anybody else I knew of. Those golden sparks were back at his fingertips and grew as he played until both his hands glowed.

When he stopped, I applauded.

"That was wonderful!"

Did he blush? Actually blush?

"Just a little something I wrote." He ducked his head to look at his guitar strings.

"You should play more like that."

"It's funny, you know. These guitars. They're old, but none of them have been played that much." He patted the Taylor, friends with it already. "I don't think the guy who pawned this was very good, but maybe he blamed the guitar instead of just practicing more. And—" He glanced up at me through those floppy bangs. "I'm gonna be weird again."

"Go for it."

"I don't think the guitar liked him. The situation. Taking the blame. The guitar is good. Really good. He wasn't worthy." He stroked the glowing koa top. "I just hope I am."

"Time will tell." I walked around his chaise to the rim of Fred's pool so Mudcat would have to face me. He didn't look as tired as he had when he arrived. In fact, he seemed completely re-energized, as if the music had fed him, the way walking around Deep Ellum fed me.

"You want lunch? I have some leftover barbeque from the place down the street. They tell me it's the best in Dallas."

"Oh, hey, I shouldn't take up all your time like this." Mudcat looked up, noticing the sun almost overhead. A cool spring breeze ruffled his hair as he glanced all around the garden.

"I like the company." I grinned. "Musicians get better discounts when they play for me."

He grinned back. "Well, then ..." He hit another chord.

I produced the "leftover" ribs, along with iced tea, and a bowl of water and a towel, so he could wash his hands before he picked up his instruments again.

Ace, Tid, and Morsel got most of my share, slipped to them while Mudcat was busy gnawing his own bones and talking about how the history and romance of Deep Ellum had captured him as a kid, and fed his hunger for music as he grew up out west, where the venues never attracted big names. He talked about disappointing his dad by preferring band to football. How he disappeared into the guitar his mother bought him whenever his parents began to fight. He told me how he'd dreamed of coming here to play some day.

"I think there must be a special spirit in this place," he said. "Waylon used to talk about it, almost as if Deep Ellum was a person as much as a place."

"You and Waylon must be close."

Mudcat stripped the meat off the last of his ribs. "More of a dad to me than my dad was. I kept trying to sneak into his dance hall on Friday nights, when the band was better than average, until he finally gave me a job bussing tables and washing dishes."

"Can't hear much music if you're in the back, washing dishes."

"Oh, no! You don't get it. See, Waylon's doesn't have dressing rooms, so the bands would hang out at the staff table in the back corner of the kitchen before their set, or when they took a break. We'd talk. Some of them even showed me licks and stuff, once they found out I was interested. And I could always sneak out front if I really wanted to hear somebody play. It was great!"

So we talked about musicians, many of whom had passed through Deep Ellum on their way to Austin, or Nashville, or New Orleans. The next thing I knew, he was pumping me for details about the musicians I'd known "growing up." I had to choose my words carefully so my memories matched my apparent age. More than once I had to fall back on the fiction that I had heard my stories from older people who had lived here back in the day.

And all the while, once the food was gone and his hands were clean again, he played. Some on the Strat, some on the Gretsch, but mostly on that little Taylor, cradled in his lap. His fingers flowed over the strings as the words flowed between us, with no conscious thought on Mudcat's part, until the energies merged into a continuous stream. I realized I was hearing the unique musical voice I hadn't heard in his concert the night before. This, the music gushing out of the man and the guitar in my garden, was the authentic Mudcat Randall.

If I didn't bother to eat again for weeks, I would still be sated.

After a while his words and his music began to slow. His eyelids drooped, until I saw he had fallen asleep, his fingers still finding chords all up the Taylor's neck.

He needed his rest. That much was clear. He'd said at the start that he hadn't slept all night. I put a little energy over his new equipment to discourage anyone from even thinking about stealing it, then tucked him up into his own little pocket of time and space where he could sleep as long as he needed. When he woke, he'd be back at Sons of Hermann with all his new gear, moments before Tim, Tico, and Nick showed up. He'd have a clear memory of saying good-bye to me and moving his stuff to the venue.

Then I left him to sleep while I fussed around in the storeroom, leafing through layers of time to put each guitar back where it belonged. When I checked the garden a few hours later, Mudcat was gone.

Cold Shot

Chapter Six

The crowd was definitely bigger at Sons of Hermann Hall for the Mudcat Randall Band's second concert. People I had seen the night before were all back, many with at least one friend in tow.

I let them flow past me, listening to the conversations that whirled by on rising gusts of excitement.

"You gotta hear this guy . . ."

"I swear, you're gonna love it."

". . . headed to South by Southwest next week. I might have to go down . . ."

"Trust me . . ."

There were a lot of women in the crowd, tripping along after their men or in tight knots of female friends. They all seemed to be wearing something low-cut, sparkly, or tight. Many of them had that on-the-hunt gleam in their eyes that said they were hoping for a good concert and an even better after party.

"He's soooo . . ."

"I heard he was . . ."

"God, I wish . . ."

The Grand Ballroom was close to capacity when I slipped inside, although I had no trouble creating a place to sit that gave me a perfect view of the stage. I scanned the instruments.

Tim had replaced his pathetic rig with a black Fender Bassman amp and a new P-Bass in candy apple red to match Tico's drums. Tico, who had apparently left his equipment onstage overnight, had added two new toms to his setup, a second bass drum, at least three cymbals, and a long row of graduated bar chimes.

Amid all that black and red, Mudcat's tobacco burst Strat, mahogany Gretsch resonator, and tweed amp glowed like the sun.

The band waited in the corner, with Nick's musclemen shielding the musicians from the audience. A few minutes before downbeat, the roar of conversation fell to a low hum of anticipation as the last stragglers found their seats. Then the muscle stepped back and the band took the stage.

They were all wearing matching outfits, like some 1950s western band: black boots and jeans, red pearl snap shirts with black piping, and a red and black bandanna. Tico's bandanna was tied around his neck. Tim had fashioned his into a do-rag to cover his stringy ginger hair. Mudcat had kept his comfy old boots. He stuffed his bandanna into his back pocket as he stepped up onto the stage and reached for his new Strat.

He scanned the crowd as he fastened his guitar strap. When he spotted me, he broke out that grin, and I couldn't help smiling back.

Then he broadcast the grin, sharing it with the whole room, and they responded with a cheer.

"You ready for some music tonight?" he asked.

The cheers got louder.

"You ready for some blues tonight?" He drew out the word.

They cheered again. Some whistled. I could feel the energy start to spark.

I glanced at Nick and saw him smiling.

Was he boosting the energy? He could, of course. It was one of his standard tricks for seducing people—singers, audiences, mass mobs at political rallies and riots. I could feel thin threads of excitement rolling off him and weaving through the crowd. But there was another energy in the hall as well, and it didn't feel like Nick's. I knew it wasn't mine.

I scanned the crowd, considering.

Then Mudcat hit the first chords of *Pride and Joy* and the audience roared. The band launched into a steady shuffle beat under him, and people all over the room started to move. Feet stomped. Shoulders swayed. One reed thin young woman stood up, shook back her jangling bracelets, and began to dance in place.

Mudcat tore through the central guitar solo, paying homage to Stevie Ray Vaughan, but making it his own this time. Sparks shot out from his strings wherever his long fingers touched them. As the people applauded, he swung into the next song on his set list, and the sparks merged into a glittering haze over his hands. Four songs later, that haze gilded his entire guitar.

I glanced at Nick again. He was focused on Mudcat the way a hungry wolf tracks every movement of his intended prey. The crazy, joyful new energy I'd detected earlier bounced back and forth between the band and the audience, building to incendiary levels. I was suddenly sharply aware that we were in a very old wood frame building, and Nick's element of choice was fire.

I took a deep breath and began to calm the crowd. I met some resistance—mostly, but not entirely, from Nick.

Mudcat didn't look my way, but he must have caught my

vibe because he unhooked the strap on the Strat and reached for his new resonator.

"We're gonna slow it down for a little while," he told the audience. "So, if you can, reach out to the one you love, 'cause love's the bluest blues you can get."

It took me a moment to recognize the next song as the original one he'd played for me in the garden, stretched out and scraped raw over the biscuit cone of the resonator guitar. No lyrics. He kept it instrumental and let the deep ache of longing come through in the music alone.

It caught the audience up in its throbbing rhythm and minor chords. Some who were still standing began to slow-dance in place, holding their partners close and swaying.

A spear of anger lanced through the crowd from Nick's corner of the room, but that odd, unknown energy snuffed it out like cold water on a match. Mudcat launched into Keb Mo's *She Just Wants to Dance,* and waves of love began to flow between the band and its fans.

Slowly, skillfully, Mudcat brought the people back to a place of harmony and peace. Tim and Tico hung in there with him although, from the glances they exchanged, I was pretty sure Mudcat had struck off into unknown territory, far from the pre-arranged set list.

The energy began to build again, song by song, as Mudcat switched back to the Strat and kicked off *Cold Shot.* His rhythms grew more insistent, building up to *Key to the Highway.* Unlike the night before, this time he turned it into a clap-along. The audience laughed with him as he reminded them that, "Friends don't let friends clap on one and three."

He brought it all to a close with the wild, irresistible joy of *Taylor's Rock.* The audience was on its feet, dancing. They barely paused to catch their breath before breaking into applause, whistles, and shouts of "More! More! More!"

"Okay, I got one more for you." The golden glow flickered like lightning all around his head and shoulders as Mudcat hit a familiar lick. "Because Deep Ellum has been so good to me."

When he ripped into the old, traditional *Deep Ellum Blues,* I thought the audience might come unglued.

Instead, as he nodded to them, they began to sing along.

"Oh, sweet mama, Daddy's got them Deep Ellum Blues!"

Not even I could resist joining in on that chorus.

"Yeah!" He raised his arms in triumph as the song ended. His golden aura rolled out from the stage to encompass the whole room.

The crowd screamed back, exultant.

And I knew, in that instant, why Nick was so desperate to get Mudcat under contract.

My head whipped around. Nick was squirming in his seat, the only one in the house not on his feet, applauding.

"Y'all think we're ready for South by Southwest?" Mudcat cried.

The cheer was deafening.

Nick pulled out his red silk pocket square to mop his brow.

"What's our name?"

"Mudcat Randall!" the audience screamed.

"Tim Reynolds, on bass!" Mudcat pointed as Tim took a bow and the people cheered.

"Tico Andrews on drums!" Mudcat stepped aside so Tico could hit a lick in acknowledgement of the crowd's roar.

Nick inched forward in his chair, tensing to stand.

"And I'm Mudcat Randall. We'll see you all in Austin!"

The crowd surged toward the stage, eager for an autograph, a handshake, a kiss. I threw a quick protective bubble over the equipment, before the fans could make off with picks, drumsticks, even the amps and instruments.

Nick shot to the front of the stage an instant before the

crowd closed in, talking fast and holding them back while the band handed gear off to the two musclebound security-guys-turned-roadies.

As the last of the instruments disappeared into the shadows, Nick raised his arms and the people froze in place.

That was an infringement on their free will, no matter how crazed they might be.

I shorted out his hold on them even as I spread calm and reason over the raging fans.

A smile flashed across Nick's face.

All the lights went out.

Somebody screamed.

I had the power back up in an instant, but Nick, Mudcat, and the band were gone, leaving only the faintest whiff of brimstone behind.

The audience gasped. They turned in circles, confused. Started rushing toward the stairs.

Frantic to find Mudcat, I still had a responsibility to get my people safely out and preserve the building if I could.

I knew what Nick had done. He doesn't have my facility for creating pockets of time and space, but he does have one trick that tends in that direction.

Nick had created a Crossroad. The Mudcat Randall Band was trapped inside.

In the Bubble

Chapter Seven

I found them in the intersection of Elm and MLK. They were suspended in Nick's Crossroad space, like figures in a snow globe, just a little above the streams of people and cars leaving the concert hall and headed for the bars.

Mudcat and his band couldn't see this, of course. I had to shed my corporeal form to see it myself. Although the Crossroad was in Deep Ellum, it was not technically *of* Deep Ellum. It did not touch my ground, nor did it contain anything from my domain. I could see in, but I could not *get* in. There was nothing I could do to stop what happened inside.

Nick's little way of kicking metaphorical dirt in my eyes, I suppose.

As I rose to prowl the perimeter, I discovered I could see the action from each band member's perspective. Tico seemed to think he was in a fancy cigar bar, lush with polished brass and leather upholstery. He sat back in his club chair, sucking on a fat perfecto, smirking at the drama unfolding between Nick, Tim, and Mudcat.

As I had suspected, Tico was already under Nick's management.

Mudcat and Tim saw something different. To them, the Crossroad was a nice office, with framed band posters on the wall and a reassuring view of the green neon Bank of America Plaza building just west of Deep Ellum, in downtown Dallas. Nick sat behind a sleek slate and chrome desk, while Tim perched on the edge of one of the guest chairs. Mudcat paced behind the chairs, hands dug into his pockets, head down as he listened. Little flickers of golden energy still sparked and fizzed around him.

Nick talked them through the various clauses of his standard "Rich and Famous" contract, his voice oily with reassurance. He listened patiently while Mudcat barked out questions about percentages, management fees, and escape clauses. Nick's answers skated above his contempt, but it was under there—as if Mudcat was a completely unsophisticated country boy to even think it was necessary to discuss such things. Of course, Nick's cut was the industry standard. Naturally Mudcat could terminate the contract if ever he chose to. He could certainly make it a personal management contract, rather than one that covered the whole band.

I knew Nick was lying. I could see it in his eyes. Hear it in his voice.

Could Mudcat?

Holding the band members in a Crossroad like this was a form of kidnapping, and the antithesis of allowing them free will. Frustrated that I couldn't intervene, I turned to some simple business on the ground.

Nick's goons were just now pulling out of the alley behind Sons of Hermann Hall. I poofed Mudcat's guitars, amp, and duffle bag from the back of their truck.

Mudcat's van, which he had driven to my pawn shop that

morning, was also parked in that alley. I put his stuff in the back, moved the van to a spot just outside my garden gate, and wrapped it in so much protective energy not even Nick would want to go back there.

By the time I'd taken care of all that, Nick was oozing to the end of his contract explanation.

When he finished, he looked up from the pages to smile at Mudcat and Tim. When neither of them had any questions, Nick slid a copy of the contract across the desk.

I don't think Tim gave it a second thought before he snatched up the pen Nick offered.

Mudcat stepped forward, half-raised a hand, and opened his mouth, but no words came out. He might have wanted to stop his lifelong friend, but he had no power to do so.

Tim signed with a flourish. If the ink looked red instead of black, he probably thought that was just rock and roll.

He added the date, tossed the pen onto the desk, and slid back in his chair, grinning. Then he looked around the office as if he expected the groupies to arrive immediately.

Mudcat shook his head.

"C'mon, old buddy. What are you waiting for?" Tim laughed up at Mudcat. "This is what we've dreamed of our whole lives, right? No more crappy little clubs. No more getting stiffed for our cut of the door. We're in the big leagues now. All you have to do is sign."

"What if I don't?" Mudcat tilted his head, narrowed his eyes, looking at Nick as if he wasn't quite sure what he saw. I remembered what he'd said about sometimes seeing two levels of reality at once. What could Mudcat see beneath Nick's slick surface layer? Would it be enough to frighten him away from that contract?

"Well . . ." Nick sounded as if he'd never heard of such a thing before. "You can, of course, find your own, personal management, but that would put a real strain on the band. I'd only be responsible for the two of them, and you and your management team might . . . I mean . . . It could threaten the cohesion of the group. I'd hate to see your band break up."

"Yeah, man, I'm your best friend and forever bass player, remember?" Tim had joined Tico in the cigar bar illusion. Rocked back in his club chair with a stogie and a snifter of brandy, he puffed a smoke ring in Mudcat's direction.

Mudcat frowned at Tim, then turned back to Nick. His golden energy seemed dimmer, somehow. It looked like he was weakening. "Can I have a night to think it over?"

Nick shook his head. "One time offer, my friend."

"Just sign it, Clyde. What is wrong with you?" Tim sneered when he used Mudcat's real name.

And I spotted a tiny thread of that golden energy worming its way across the floor from Mudcat's boot to one of Nick's polished Gucci loafers.

I saw now what I'd only suspected during the concert: Nick wanted Mudcat under contract for the energy.

Nick and I are ethereal beings. We feed off the energy of the world—energy that is neither created nor destroyed, merely shared and transformed. What I'd realized, back at Sons of Hermann Hall, was that Mudcat had a talent for getting people to share their energy. He gave them his, though his music. They paid him back a hundred times over as they clapped, danced, sang, fell in love, got over heartbreak, and opened themselves to joy in response.

That third energy, pushing back against both Nick's attempts to control the crowd and mine? That was Mudcat. It was his crowd to control, and the waves of energy that lit up his golden aura were what he'd said he'd sell his soul to feel.

It created a different sort of high, that energy. More natural and sustaining than any drug. If Mudcat signed with Nick, he'd get artificially boosted levels of that audience response. Higher highs, but also deeper lows as Nick took his "management fee" by draining Mudcat.

The way he was draining him now, causing Mudcat to crash prematurely, confused and uncertain about what was actually going on.

Trapping Mudcat in a Crossroad and draining his energy piled up violation on violation. Not that I ever expected Nick to play fair.

There was no way I could explain any of this to Mudcat as long as I was locked out of the Crossroad.

I batted against the outer boundary in frustration, and lightning streaked around the perimeter. Mudcat turned his head to watch.

"It's storming? When did it start to storm?"

"Never mind that." Nick offered the contract to Mudcat again.

But Mudcat turned away from Nick, frowning at the walls of the Crossroad as I sent another pulse of lightning around them.

Mudcat looked from the sunny view out the office windows behind Nick to the cozy cigar bar where Tim and Tico talked and laughed too quietly now to hear. He turned all the way around, studying the "office wall" where I had struck it.

Had I created a thin spot, where the illusion didn't hold as well? Could he see me, just outside?

"What is this place?"

"Forget this place." Nick, pumped on Mudcat's energy, was running out of patience. "Just sign the damned contract."

"I want to understand."

"No, you don't. You want to be a rock star. A blues legend." Nick didn't quite control his sneer. "And I can make that happen for you. If you sign."

"No."

Mudcat turned his back on Nick and walked across the office to what must have looked like a door to him. He made several futile grabs at the doorknob before whirling back to Nick.

"What *is* this place?"

"You want to know where you are?" Nick rose from the desk, little flames flickering around him, burning hot from Mudcat's energy. "*This* is where you are!"

Smoke billowed up and the scene changed. Dallas was gone. The office, the club, all the illusions of comfort were gone. Mudcat stood alone at the place where two narrow, unpaved roads crossed before the gate of a small pioneer cemetery. A wrought iron arch rose above the gate, with blocky black letters spelling out CROSSROADS, just in case Mudcat hadn't gotten the point.

Mudcat staggered back, coughing. He raised his arms to shield his face from the smoke and flames.

"I want to leave. Now."

"You think you can do that?" Nick stalked toward Mudcat, not swerving around a fancy corporate desk, but moving straight ahead between the old and crooked tombstones of the cemetery. "Do you really think you have the power to walk away when I am offering you everything you said you ever wanted?"

Nick's face shifted into a leaner, older version of Mudcat's own face. "You don't have the balls to walk away. You're weak. You always were a weakling!"

"No!" Mudcat backed away another step, but the ground rolled and shuddered under his feet. "No! Stop it! Get away!"

Mudcat was gasping now, from smoke or panic, or some combination of both. Lightning split the clouds, and thunder bounced all around the walls of the Crossroad.

"You're pathetic!" Nick advanced on Mudcat, unphased by storm or earthquake. "You're a disgrace! Sign the contract! Or don't expect to come around whining for help when you're destitute. You're a failure. You've always been a failure. I'm the only one who can help you succeed!"

Cold rain sluiced down on Mudcat as he sank to his knees. Wind whipped bits of grass and dirt into his eyes until he had to cower to cover them.

I smacked the outer wall of the Crossroad one more time, my frustration building as my lightning streaked past Mudcat again, unseen in the explosion of power and thunder within. Power Nick was drawing from Mudcat himself. As he grew stronger, Mudcat weakened.

I wanted to scream. I wanted to rage. I wanted to blow that horrible Crossroad out of the sky. But I couldn't risk the people passing peacefully below, and I had no idea what would happen to Mudcat inside his bubble if I tried.

"You're nothing! Nothing!" Nick towered over Mudcat now, still wearing the face I guessed was his father's. His teeth became fangs, tipped with fire, and the smoke billowed out of his mouth. "You'll never amount to anything unless you sign the contract!

Mudcat's shoulders began to shake, and I heard his broken sob.

"You want to make your father proud? You want to stand up and be a man?" Nick's foot swung out, kicking Mudcat in the ribs, and nearly tipping him over. "Stand up. Stand up and be a man! Grab hold of your dreams. You're too stupid to see your opportunity. You're too weak to actually reach for what you said you always wanted."

"No! Help! Help me!" Mudcat's voice was barely a whimper.

Nick bent down to grab Mudcat's arm.

"Help me!" Mudcat arched back, screaming and convulsing, as if he had been touched by a live power line. "Help me, Miss Eddy! HELP ME!"

Not even Nick could keep me out when a soul in need invoked my help.

The protective bubble of the Crossroad shattered around me when I burst through. Nick, Tico, and Tim tumbled away into chaos as I wrapped Mudcat in my arms and snapped both of us back to the safety of my garden.

New Way to Pray

Chapter Eight

We crash-landed into Fred's pool, which left both of us wet and dripping. I began to laugh as I staggered out of the shallow salt-water sea, but Mudcat was still confused.

"Wha—What?" He swiped his hair away from his eyes, then doubled over, coughing up water.

"Come on." I reached back, grabbed his hand, and hauled him out of the water as Ace, Tid, and Morsel emerged from the shop to see what all the fuss was about. Deep in the pool, Fred lashed his tail, bumping Mudcat's boot, but not biting.

"It's okay." I coaxed Mudcat up the sloping shore. "You're safe now."

"You—You came." He staggered onto the stones of the patio and collapsed into the chaise he'd occupied when he selected his guitars.

Had that only been this morning?

"You invoked me."

"Invoked. Ha." Mudcat was still panting a little as I waved

the water from his hair and clothing, as well as my own. "Waylon said you'd be there if I needed you."

"Waylon knows his stuff." I perched on the edge of the other chaise, leaning toward him. "How do you feel?"

He snorted and shook his head. "Like I've been run over by a train. That was trapped in a tornado." He swung his legs up onto the chaise and leaned back. "What happened?"

"What do you remember?"

He closed his eyes. "I remember that the concert was good. The audience was good. We had a nice vibe going. And I remember that you were there. Ashton." He sat up abruptly and looked down at his clothes. The black jeans and red pearl snap shirt were clean, dry, and perfectly pressed.

"Ashton gave us all these dorky clothes. Said they would make us look professional. Like a real band, not some random collection of college kids. I didn't want to wear them."

"You looked like escapees from the Porter Wagoner show."

"Hey!" His smile still looked a little shell-shocked. "You know about Porter? Not so many people do, anymore."

"Eclectic musical tastes. What else do you remember?"

He cocked his head, his eyes roaming the garden, but clearly focused on his memories, not his immediate surroundings. "We . . . finished up. Did the encore. *Deep Ellum Blues*." He peered up at me through those floppy bangs. "That was for you. I didn't get the chance to dedicate it, but I thought you might know anyway."

"I appreciate that. It was a great concert. One of my all-time favorites."

"And then after that . . ." He shook his head. "It's just weird. After the concert, everything got weird."

"Tell me."

He squinted a little.

"I'm not going to think you're crazy. I promise."

"Well . . . it was like all of a sudden, I wasn't at Sons of Hermann anymore. I was . . . we were all in this office somewhere. Downtown Dallas, I guess. I could see the green building. And Ashton was asking us to sign a management contract, but . . . it just didn't seem right, somehow. He didn't seem right. I looked at him, and he looked like Ashton but . . . like . . . under his skin, I could see snakes crawling. And I promise I hadn't taken any drugs. It wasn't a bad trip or anything like that. Unless he . . ."

"He didn't. You should trust yourself, those times when you see different levels of reality. It's not a hallucination. It's a skill."

He inhaled sharply, held the breath a long moment, then slowly blew it back out again. "Is he the Devil?"

"Yes."

"Jesus!" Mudcat sat bolt upright and slewed around to stare at me. "Just that simple? The Devil? For real?"

"Where did he take you?"

"To . . . to this . . ." He looked up at me, frowning. Remembering. "He took me to the crossroads. Like in that Robert Johnson song. He wanted me to sign a management contract."

"Any major decision or turning point in your life can be a metaphorical crossroad. Which way do you turn? Where do you decide to go?"

"But that contract . . . he wanted me to sell my soul?"

"Not so many people do, anymore." I smoothed out some non-existent wrinkles in my shirt. "Nick can always pick up random bits of evil energy in the world. Plenty of wars. Plenty of violence. But not as many people believe in him the way they did back in the Dark Ages. Not too many people consciously pledge their lives to him these days." I shrugged. "Blues guys still believe. They believe in Robert Johnson, and that deal he made with the Devil. Some of them—the hungry ones—want to make that deal for fame and fortune themselves."

Ace, who had been listening from the shadows, edged forward at my mention of Robert Johnson. He rested his large black head on Mudcat's knee. Those long, talented fingers automatically began to stroke Ace between the ears.

"Do I have to worry about Hell Hounds on my trail now?" Mudcat half laughed at the idea.

"You didn't sign." I smiled. "So he'll mostly leave you alone unless you start slipping him lots of treats."

Mudcat froze. "Wait. What?" He looked from Ace to me and back again.

Ace nudged his hand impatiently.

"Long story. You stopped petting him."

His hand began to move again. "Is that my fate now? To spend my years petting a Hell Hound?"

I laughed and waved the idea away. "Sooner or later he'll take a nap."

Mudcat lifted his free hand to massage his forehead. "This has been the strangest night of my life."

I stood up. "Are you hungry?"

"Not really." He reached up, took my hand, rose from the chaise. "Will he come back?"

"Nick? Yes. If you invite him. If you decide that's what you want."

"To be a rock star?" Mudcat turned away, pacing the length of Fred's pool. "To have all the fame and fortune a man could ask for? And then what? Die tragically at the peak of my success? Become an immortal only after I'm gone?"

I shrugged again. "It happens."

"Too often." Slowly he walked back to me, still thinking. Still trying to figure it out. "Unless . . . " He shook his head. "I don't want to be a rock star."

He reached for my hand again, stroking it as he had stroked Ace a moment ago. His fingers played gentle rhythms over mine, soothing, stirring, sending little jolts of energy up my arm.

"What do you want?" My voice was little more than a whisper.

"I want to be a good musician." He moved subtly closer. "I want to learn how to play—really play—those great guitars you sold me. I want to win my audiences the honest way, with good music and real talent."

He slipped his other hand around my waist. "And I want to find a goddess who will lead me toward the light, not the darkness."

He bent his head until his lips whispered over mine. "Someone who will be there when I need her."

I tilted my head to meet him. The kiss was sweet and soft.

"I just want to worship you." He kissed me again, more strongly now. That energy Nick had been so eager to steal sang through my bones.

"Please. Let me worship you?"

What was I supposed to do? Tell him no?

Sunday Morning Coming Down
Chapter Nine

We might have started out on our feet, but it wasn't long before we hit the horizontal in a little pocket of time and space masquerading as a well-appointed bedroom. By the time we took a breather, that golden glow had spread from Mudcat's fingers to encompass his whole, very manly body, and he had demonstrated a vocal range that stretched from a low blues growl to fervent hallelujahs of grateful praise.

I stirred as the sun rose. Mudcat lay beside me, still naked and deeply asleep.

"Time to get up, lover."

"Not sure that's physically possible." He nuzzled more deeply into his pillow.

I ran light fingers down his belly to his legs, feeling him stir in response.

"Your body says you're lying."

"Awww, man . . ." He rolled onto his back, his eyes still closed. "Okay. Gimme a minute."

I straddled him briefly as I slipped out of bed. "I'll give you a break, this time."

He snatched at my leg but missed, proving he still had some reflexes, but they weren't fully recovered.

It took him the better part of an hour to straggle down the back stairs of the pawn shop and find me in my garden. Ace slept by my side, but Morsel and Tid were busy stalking bees among the wildflowers.

The sun had just crept over the garden wall. Mudcat, back in his comfy boots and new black jeans, squinted at it as he stretched and yawned. He wore his red pearl snap shirt, but it hung open over his chest.

"Mornin', lover." I waved at the platter of fruit and muffins on the table between our chaises. "I won't ask if you slept well."

"And yet I feel strangely energized." He scooped up a blue-berry muffin as he dropped onto the chaise opposite me.

A pot of hot coffee materialized on the table. He raised an eyebrow at me.

"So. Not much of a cook?"

"I may not need to eat again for years."

"Mmmm." He bit into the muffin. "You're welcome."

Deep in his pocket, his phone pinged. He crammed the last bite of muffin into his mouth and dug for the phone.

"Text from Tim." He squinted at his screen. "Looks like I'm a loser."

"Unlikely."

"They've already found a much better lead guitar to replace me."

"Doubt he's better, but I'm sure Nick has lead guitar players stacked to the ceiling in a warehouse somewhere. Are they keeping the band's name?"

"Nope. Changing it to TNT Blues Band. New guy's name is Nestor."

"Cute." At least Nick wasn't trying to steal Mudcat's name.

"Aaaand, they're taking my showcase slot at South by Southwest."

"I'm sure." I rolled a little in his direction so I could watch his face. "Will you be okay with it, if this turns out to be their big breakthrough performance? If their first record is a megahit?"

He seemed to consider it for a moment, then shrugged. His eyes were bluer than blue when they met mine.

"One-hit wonders," he said.

"That happens."

He swung his legs over the side of chaise, found a mug when he looked for it, and poured himself some coffee. "The thing is, Eddy, it's a marathon, not a sprint." He blew across the steam rising from his cup. "If I can play, if I can learn, if I can make people happy, I'm a success. At least to myself. If I have fans? That's gravy."

"What's your next step, then?"

"Ah." He took a sip, but the coffee was still too hot. "Find my van and figure out what Ashton—sorry—Nick—did with my gear, I guess."

"Van's out back. Gear's inside." I nodded toward the garden gate.

His eyebrows shot up. "Merch, too?"

I paused a moment, located the dumpster where Nick's goons had tossed his tee shirts, bumper stickers, and CDs. Moved them—sanitized—to the back of his van. "Merch, too."

"Wow." He stood, bent down to kiss me. "You *are* a goddess."

"Never doubt it."

I let him finish his coffee before suggesting a dip in Fred's pool.

Time wandered around for a while, but eventually we hauled ourselves out of the water, retrieved one of his merch shirts to replace the shredded red pearl snap number that no longer had any snaps, and Mudcat made a reluctant move to leave.

"Where you headed next?" I watched him open the back of the van to check the condition of everything in there.

"Austin." He shoved the merch box and the amp aside to pull the hardshell Strat case forward.

"I may not have the showcase slot, but I still have a pass and a hotel room." He opened the case and inspected the Strat, fret by fret, then latched it all down again and reached for the resonator.

"I figure I can still listen. Learn new stuff. Meet new people." He checked out the Taylor acoustic, too, then backed out of the cargo hold and sat on the sill.

"Come with me?"

I walked forward until I was standing between his legs. "You know I can't."

His hands settled on my waist. "I'll never forget you."

"You'd better not."

He stretched up as I bent down. Our kiss met in the middle.

"Now I understand why Waylon always spoke of Deep Ellum as a woman."

I nibbled, just a little, along his jawline. "You're welcome back, any time."

"But?" He cocked his head to one side.

I stepped away.

"But now it's time I get out there." He nodded. "Figure out who I am on this side of the crossroad. Spend a lot more hours in the woodshed until I find that sound I've been reaching for."

I smiled, looking him over from head to toe as he hopped down and locked up the back of the van. Maybe I put a little more "don't steal this" mojo on it, but I figured he'd get the hang of that himself before too long.

We had shared a lot of energy all through the night. That kind of exchange weaves strands of each lover deep into the other's soul.

The golden glow that had been little more than a flicker when I first saw him had grown into a full-length aureole that shone strong and bright from his tousled hair to his scuffed-up boots.

And I knew, beyond any doubt, what I had made of him in our time together.

A brand shiny new guitar god.

—The End—

Mudcat's Set Lists

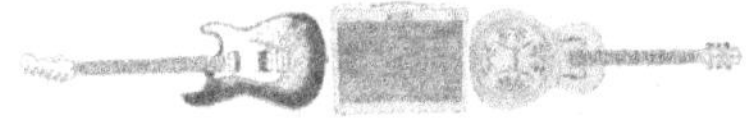

Friday Night's Set

Pride and Joy (Stevie Ray Vaughan)
https://youtu.be/ovo23H9J8o8

Key to the Highway (B. B. King)
https://youtu.be/zDCXXSasyoo
This is a Little Walter song, but most folks know it from the recording with B. B. King and Eric Clapton, which is what I have included here. Freddy King recorded it. Sonny Landreth recorded it. Just about any blues guy worth his salt has played it. You've got to figure Mudcat knows all the versions out there.

If you're curious about what a resonator guitar sounds like, check out Sonny Landreth's version.

https://youtu.be/ce2peVon7oI

Hideaway (Freddy King)
https://youtu.be/wEmGbMd2duk

Stevie Ray Vaughan also has a killer version of this on his *Couldn't Stand the Weather* recording.
https://youtu.be/3FodSPqPnpU for Stevie Ray Vaughan.

Born Under a Bad Sign (Albert King)
https://youtu.be/2Py37G9qsfY

Wild About You Baby (Hound Dog Taylor)
https://youtu.be/K-uw7iU9-3E

Black Snake Moan (Blind Lemon Jefferson)
https://youtu.be/XsrRUdCwJew
Blind Lemon Jefferson was one of the early influencers of the musical style we now call the blues. He played in Deep Ellum and around Texas as "the blues" was coming into focus. This recording is the raw and real deal, recorded during the days when Jefferson was playing in the clubs and street corners of Deep Ellum. Somewhat improbably, Jimmie Dale Gilmore recorded a version on his *Braver, Newer World* record. Check it out and see how he preserves some of Jefferson's guitar licks.
https://youtu.be/Zm9LzK3nQzs

They Call It Stormy Monday (T-Bone Walker)
https://youtu.be/BpK2GDUbXv8
T-Bone Walker was a pioneer in using an electronic pickup to amplify his guitar. Although he is generally associated with the Chicago blues sound, he was born in Linden, Texas, and

spent his early years gigging in and around Dallas. His parents played in the kind of string band Henry and Rosalie Wilson, from *Deep Ellum Pawn,* would have played in, and were familiar figures in the emerging blues scene in Deep Ellum in the 1920s. It is said that Blind Lemon Jefferson used to drop by for Sunday dinner at Walker's home. T-Bone himself played in a number of bands in and around the Deep Ellum and Oak Cliff neighborhoods of Dallas, honing his chops before he headed out to Los Angeles, then Chicago, for a recording contract and wider recognition of his talents.

Hellhound on My Trail (Robert Johnson)
https://youtu.be/G2URlDdDTMo

Miz Eddy has some experience with Hellhounds, herself.

Stone Crazy (Buddy Guy)
https://youtu.be/SK1vkls4Kjg

City Boy (Keb' Mo)
https://youtu.be/wM-OSUHjt6o

Somebody's Gotta Make a Move (Sonny Landreth)
https://youtu.be/uNaDDbZck7U
This song was written by Steve Conn, a frequent collaborator of Sonny's. I pretty much figure we've all been there.

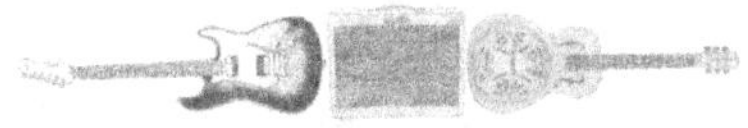

Saturday Night's Set List

Pride and Joy (Stevie Ray Vaughan)
https://youtu.be/ovo23H9J8o8

Four unidentified songs—so pick your four favorites from Friday night!

Original Song, which has no name and certainly no video.

She Just Wants to Dance (Keb' Mo')
https://youtu.be/m43MfixAIq4

Cold Shot (Stevie Ray Vaughan)
https://youtu.be/-CixtG_bF28

Key to the Highway (B. B. King)
https://youtu.be/zDCXXSasyoo

Taylor's Rock (Hound Dog Taylor via Sonny Landreth)
https://youtu.be/byqeKTrgCto
You can find Hound Dog Taylor's version of this song on YouTube, but I selected Sonny Landreth's version because a) it's a little cleaner and b) it's Sonny. He's my own personal guitar god, although not in any way akin to the way Miz Eddy might mean it.

Deep Ellum Blues (Jimmie Dale Gilmore and the Wronglers)
https://youtu.be/RFPPjNtkMDA
There are a jillion covers of this traditional blues song, from Doc Watson to the Grateful Dead to Jimmie Dale Gilmore. Some take it slow. Doc Watson takes it almost fast enough to be a fiddle tune. I've picked the Jimmie Dale Gilmore version

because a) I like Jimmie Dale Gilmore, b) I like his chosen tempo, and c) the audio is clear. But, by all means, go out there and search for more versions. Doc Watson's is a classic; the Dead made it famous even if they can't spell; and the Blackberry Smoke version with Billy Gibbons is pretty cool, too.

Acknowledgments

I have hung around with musicians for most of my adult life and have worked everything from intimate house concerts to lavish events at symphony halls. I am not, however, much of a musician myself. I have a number of excellent shade-tree pickers, blues guys, and professional recording artists to thank for the background information on the Mudcat Randall Band's gear, including Matthew Broyles, Levi Ray, and all the guys who hung out over the years at Craig's Music in Weatherford Texas. My Dallas Winds colleague, Todd Toney, gave me some of the vocabulary I needed to describe the music. My adopted brother-in-law, Gerald Ray, gave me the detailed rundown on amps and vintage guitars. The incomparable Guy Forsyth outlined Mudcat's dream rig for me. Thanks, guys! I love you all. Any deviation from the truth comes from me, not them.

I am so fortunate to have had Deborah Crombie as my critique partner for the better part of twenty years and counting. She calls me on my crap, boosts me up when I want to backspace over all of it, and cheers me on whenever I finish another chapter. Thanks, Deb. You're the best.

And I must have been born lucky, because in the great Sibling Sweepstakes, I drew Jan Sherrell Gephardt. After years of mutual frustration with the publishing industry, she and I have joined forces in Weird Sisters Publishing LLC. If you are enjoying Ms. Eddy's adventures, it's due in large part to Jan, who does all the heavy lifting when it comes time to put a new book together and take it on the road. Thanks, always, Jan! Here's to our next great adventure.

About the Author

G. S. Norwood was more or less doomed to a life as an arts professional. Her mother was an art teacher and her father taught drafting and design. She was listening to classical music in the womb, and spent her summer vacations roaming art museums the way other kids went to Six Flags and Disneyland.

Since her older sister was a seriously amazing visual artist with a beautiful soprano voice, G. went into theatre and instrumental music, where there was less competition. She got her BFA in Theatre and Interpretation but dropped out of band when she realized she'd have to get up really early all summer long and march. Being a night owl with kinesthetic dyslexia, she understood that marching band would not play to her strengths.

Writing, however, was a constant. She took her first stab at storytelling when she was four. The story didn't have a strong plot, and the characters were a little sketchy, but it had something to do with horses and ghosts—subjects she still enjoys.

As a professional, she has written political speeches, press releases, brochure copy, radio commercials, and feature stories for a major regional newspaper. After a stint in the corporate healthcare world she fled home to the arts, writing grant proposals for the Van Cliburn Foundation, the Dallas Symphony Orchestra, and many others. She is currently back on the production side of the desk as Director of Concert Operations for the Dallas Winds.

Married for seventeen years to writer Warren C. Norwood, she has written a number of novels, short stories, and blog posts. *Deep Ellum Duet* grew out of her affection for the Deep Ellum neighborhood of Dallas, Texas, and her working knowledge of musical instruments, regional folklore, and all the other odd bits of stuff that have piled up in that store room behind the pawnshop.

What to Read Next?

We hope you enjoyed G. S. Norwood's urban fantasy "Duet" of novellas!

If you did, please give this book a star-rating on **Goodreads**, **Amazon**, or **wherever you purchased this book**. A review helps even more!

While we all wait for **_Death in Deep Ellum_** (in progress now) perhaps you'll enjoy these other Weird Sisters Publishing productions!

L-R: **The Other Side of Fear,** *cover art © 2020 by Lucy A. Synk;* **What's Bred in the Bone,** *and* **A Bone to Pick,** *cover art © 2019 and 2020, respectively, by Jody A. Lee.*

Jan S. Gephardt's XK9 Stories

XK9s are uplifted police dogs on a space station. They solve crimes and sniff out bad guys in these science fiction mysteries. Read more details on the **Weird Sisters Publishing** website, where you'll find longer descriptions and links to many fine booksellers who offer these books.

The Other Side of Fear

Officer Pam Gómez has big dreams, a doubtful boyfriend, and a tiny flat.

But she's headed for XK9 training on Planet Chayko. Can big dreams and a giant dog take her to the other side of fear?

More details on this book's page of the Weird Sisters Publishing website.

What's Bred in the Bone

XK9 Rex is a dog who thinks too much ... and it could get him killed.

Rex and his Packmates were bio-engineered and cyber-enhanced to be cutting edge law enforcement tools, both smart and verbal. But there's smart ... and then there's sapient. In the star systems of the Alliance of the Peoples, that's a legal distinction with potentially deadly consequences for XK9 Rex and his Pack.

Learn more on this book's page of the Weird Sisters Publishing website.

A Bone to Pick

XK9 Rex is a dog who knows too much. Now his past is gunning for him.

Rex and his bio-engineered Packmates are so smart they're considered uplifted sapient beings on Rana Habitat Space Station. Rex may be Leader of the Pack on Rana, but his past is still on his trail.

See this book's page of the Weird Sisters Publishing website for a longer description.

Bone of Contention

XK9 Rex is a dog who dreams too big. Now he may lose everything.

Rex and the Pack have begun to enjoy the freedom Ranans believe they deserve. But they also have work to do. They're hot on the trail of a murderous gang that blows up spaceships in the black void of space.

But in the far-flung systems of the Alliance of the Peoples, trafficking in sapient beings is even more deeply reviled than mass murder. The system-dominating Transmondian Government that sponsored the XK9 Project will do anything they must to protect themselves from that charge. Even if it means destroying every XK9 in the universe.

Bone of Contention is still a work in progress, set for publication in the fall of 2023 if all goes well. More details on this book's page of the Weird Sisters Publishing website.

Warren C. Norwood's *Windhover* Tetralogy

Due for release at intervals during 2023!